Final Verdict

Weakly, the wounded man raised a Schofield revolver in his shaking right hand, squinting his eyes at Hawk.

"You b-bastard." The pistol fell from his grip. "Who the hell are you?"

Hawk took his rifle in his left hand and pulled back his right lapel, revealing the moon-and-star marshal's badge pinned to his shirt.

The man's left eye slitted. *"Lawman?"*

"That's right."

The man was incredulous. "You never . . . never even gave us a chance. Ain't you supposed to give us a chance?"

"After what you did to that town, that posse, and those two girls . . ."

The man's chest rose and fell sharply. "But that's the law!"

"Not my law," Hawk said. As he took his rifle in his right hand and aimed at the man's head, the man's eyes snapped wide.

"No!"

His plea was punctuated by the explosion of Hawk's Henry . . .

ROGUE LAWMAN
DEADLY PREY

Peter Brandvold

BERKLEY BOOKS, NEW YORK

THE BERKLEY PUBLISHING GROUP
Published by the Penguin Group
Penguin Group (USA) Inc.
375 Hudson Street, New York, New York 10014, USA
Penguin Group (Canada), 90 Eglinton Avenue East, Suite 700, Toronto, Ontario M4P 2Y3 Canada
(a division of Pearson Penguin Canada Inc.)
Penguin Books Ltd., 80 Strand, London WC2R 0RL, England
Penguin Group Ireland, 25 St. Stephen's Green, Dublin 2, Ireland (a division of Penguin Books Ltd.)
Penguin Group (Australia), 250 Camberwell Road, Camberwell, Victoria 3124, Australia
(a division of Pearson Australia Group Pty. Ltd.)
Penguin Books India Pvt. Ltd., 11 Community Centre, Panchsheel Park, New Delhi—110 017, India
Penguin Group (NZ), Cnr. Airborne and Rosedale Roads, Albany, Auckland 1310, New Zealand
(a division of Pearson New Zealand Ltd.)
Penguin Books (South Africa) (Pty.) Ltd., 24 Sturdee Avenue, Rosebank, Johannesburg 2196,
South Africa

Penguin Books Ltd., Registered Offices: 80 Strand, London WC2R 0RL, England

This is a work of fiction. Names, characters, places, and incidents either are the product of the author's imagination or are used fictitiously, and any resemblance to actual persons, living or dead, business establishments, events, or locales is entirely coincidental. The publisher does not have any control over and does not assume any responsibility for author or third-party websites or their content.

ROGUE LAWMAN: DEADLY PREY

A Berkley Book / published by arrangement with the author

PRINTING HISTORY
Berkley edition / April 2006

Copyright © 2006 by Peter Brandvold.
Cover design by Steven Ferlauto.
Cover illustration by Bruce Emmett.
Interior text design by Kristin del Rosario.

ISBN: 0-425-20915-6

BERKLEY®
Berkley Books are published by The Berkley Publishing Group,
a division of Penguin Group (USA) Inc.,
375 Hudson Street, New York, New York 10014.
BERKLEY is a registered trademark of Penguin Group (USA) Inc.
The "B" design is a trademark belonging to Penguin Group (USA) Inc.

PRINTED IN THE UNITED STATES OF AMERICA

10 9 8 7 6 5 4 3 2 1

For my uncle and aunt, Vernon and Loueen Meyer

1.

FARO MAN

"WHERE'VE I seen you before, hombre?"

"Mister, you've never seen me before."

"No, I seen you somewhere." The man on the other side of the faro box from Gideon Hawk clucked his tongue and narrowed his eyes. "Where was it, now? Let me think."

"Don't think too hard."

The man frowned at Hawk, concentrating.

"Mister, either buck the tiger, or leave. I'm not in the mood for chitchat."

"You ever deal faro in Abilene?"

"Nope."

"Deadwood?"

Hawk stared across the table at the stocky, middle-aged prospector in a plug hat, suspenders, and a red-checked shirt with a torn breast pocket. "Mister, maybe you haven't been on the frontier all that long," Hawk said, keeping his voice low and taut with menace. "Let me give you a word of advice. Sticking your nose in where it doesn't belong is liable to get your *whole body* in a pine box."

The man stared back at Hawk, his craggy face flushing all the way up to the gray curl angling down from beneath his shabby hat to his grizzled left brow. That eye twitched nervously, and the lines in his forehead planed out. "Never mind. Guess it ain't none of my business."

"There's your soda card, Mr. Donovan. Would you like to see the hoc?"

The prospector looked at the card Hawk had set over the queen of diamonds staring faceup from the faro board. The man rolled a cautious glance up at Hawk's dark, finely chiseled face, the green eyes set deep beneath a heavy brow.

Hawk's expression was sharp, cold as winter granite.

The man blinked, winced. He turned his head to look around the room.

Not much was happening. The gaunt bartender stood on a stool to reset the banjo clock over the back bar, and six or seven other rock-breakers played poker in the room's back shadows. A lone Mexican in bullhide chaps, calico shirt, and low-crowned sombrero sat alone near the piano, nursing a tequila bottle. He'd poured a small pile of salt on the table beside his shot glass. Now he brushed the top of his right hand through the pile. With the other hand, he tossed back a shot, then ran the salt across his mouth, smacking his lips with a savoring sigh.

Hawk chuffed to himself, amused.

He had been dealing faro in the saloon for the past four days. The vaquero was a lonely Mexican line rider who played the piano at night for free tequila and whatever tips he could land. The smacking sound that the man made as he drank was now as familiar to Hawk as the bartender's frequent yawns, the ticks of the clock behind the bar, the clank of the blacksmith hammer across the street, and the giggles of the girls and the squawks of their bedsprings in the second-story rooms.

There were no giggles or spring squawks at the moment, however. The drovers and vaqueros wouldn't be paid till Friday, so the two pale, sullen whores were getting their beauty sleep.

Hawk was here only because he needed a stake. When he'd made enough *dinero* for ammunition and grub, he'd head back to his cabin in the San Juans, where his chances of being recognized as the man who'd come to be known as the "Rogue Lawman" was slimmer than here in Pagosa Springs, Colorado Territory.

The prospector turned back to Hawk, his face still flushed with fear. He swallowed, placed both hands on the table, and slid his chair back. Offering a wan smile, he said, "I think I'll mosey over to the poker game yonder, try my lousy luck over there."

"That might be wise," Hawk said. The prospector had set a silver dollar on the queen of diamonds.

Hawk picked it up, tossed it into the air. "Have a couple drinks on me."

The man snatched the coin in his fist. A relieved smile grew on his face, eyes slitting agreeably. He opened his mouth to speak, but before he could get the words out, a gun popped in the street. Snapping his mouth shut, the prospector turned to the front window.

The gun popped again.

The prospector turned a wry grin to Hawk. "Sounds like some drovers made it to town early this week. Probably Don Vincente's vaqueros."

He shook his head and turned toward the poker table at the room's smoky rear. He'd taken only three steps before several more shots sounded and men began shouting down the east end of the main street. Galloping hooves thudded. A girl screamed and sobbed.

The prospector stopped and swung toward the batwings, scowling. "Hey, that ain't just no—!"

Cutting off the man's exclamation, two quick shots rose from the street before the saloon. Both slugs plunked through the front window, one whining through the air over Hawk's right shoulder and thudding into the room's back wall, evoking exclamations from the poker table.

The other bullet crunched into the prospector's chest, shoving him straight back against a post. He dropped the silver dollar as he lifted his hands to the small, round hole in his heavy wool shirt.

Hawk was up in a wink, shoving his frock coat

back from his waist and clawing his big Russian .44 from the cross-draw holster on his left hip, his boots pounding the puncheons as he bolted toward the batwings. He stopped just inside the louvered doors and looked outside as several riders passed before the saloon. They fired pistols willy-nilly at the sod-and-log or adobe buildings sheathing the street, dust and smoke sifting in their wake.

Another rider approached from Hawk's left—a lean kid with long pewter hair, a spade beard, and a high-crowned sombrero. He grinned and whooped as he rode, his right arm wrapped around the waist of a young girl who screamed and dragged her elastic-sided boots along the ground, her long, blond curls and gingham skirts whipping in the wind. A string tie bobbed beneath the rider's chin, his black duster winging out against his horse's pounding hips. He turned to fire a pistol over his left shoulder, at two men firing at him from the boardwalk fronting the bank, then whipped forward, quickly sheathing his pistol and using his left hand to pull the girl over his saddle horn.

"Don't shoot!" a woman screamed. "He's got my daughter!"

Hawk stepped onto the boardwalk and turned his head left, where the woman, clad in a stylish burnt-orange dress and matching feathered picture hat, ran toward the fleeing riders. She didn't get far before she tripped over her own skirts and fell face-first in the street. Lifting her head and staring westward along the dusty, smoky street, she screamed, *"They have Amy and the Peterson girl!"*

A tall, beefy man in a cheap suit ran up on Hawk's left, hefting a double-barreled Greener in his hands. Cursing and bunching his lips furiously, he raised the shotgun to his shoulder and, as he passed before Hawk, aimed it toward the fleeing bank robbers.

Hawk stuck his right foot out. The man tripped over it and yowled as he tumbled into the street. Both barrels of the shotgun exploded, the blast echoing off the buildings and dislodging dust from the awning over Hawk's head. The buckshot dug a deep gash in the street.

The shotgunner raised up on his hands and swung his face toward Hawk, his big, Irish features sunset-red with exasperation. "What the hell you think you're doin', mate?"

The bartender, who'd walked out behind Hawk, answered for him. "Christalmighty, Jim, you wanna hit one of those girls?"

Jim spit dust from his lips and switched his gaze to the barman. "Those bastards robbed the damn bank, Henry. Maybe you don't have any money in there, but I do!"

"Let the law take care of it," Hawk said, staring up the street where the last rider and the girl swung around a bend in the trail and disappeared.

"Law, hell!" Jim heaved himself onto his knees, then to his feet. "That four-eyed coward couldn't track a bleedin' griz through fresh snow!" He dusted himself off, picked up his shotgun, and stomped back the way he'd come, cursing and shaking his head.

Meanwhile, the woman in the burnt-orange dress had gained her own feet. She was raging at a short, bespectacled gent with long gray hair and a bowler hat who'd stooped to help a wounded man to his feet. A marshal's star glistened on his brown wool vest.

"Go after them, Marshal," the woman screamed, hatless, her hair, having come loose from its bun, hanging in tatters about her shoulders. "For God's sake, man, what're you doing? They're getting away!"

The man muttered something to the woman, then spoke to several other townsmen gathered around him, too far away for Hawk to hear the words. Holstering his .44, Gideon turned and walked back into the saloon.

Two miners who'd been gambling at the back table were crouched down beside Donovan, the prospector to whom Hawk had been dealing faro. The man sat with his back against the square-hewn joist, legs straight out before him, eyes wide and unblinking. Thick red blood ran down from the hole in the dead center of his chest.

One of the poker players was waving his hat in front of Donovan's face and peering into the man's eyes. The other held a finger to the man's neck and shook his head, muttering, "Deader'n a damn doornail, sure enough."

Hawk walked over to his table, closed his faro box, grabbed his black, flat-brimmed hat off a chair, and donned it. He turned and strode past the dead prospector and the two clucking gamblers. The other gamblers had resumed their poker, as though nothing had happened.

Hawk crossed to the back of the room and climbed the stairs leading to the second story. Less than five minutes later, he came back down, carrying a Henry rifle, saddlebags, a bedroll, and a war bag. Pushing through the batwings, he saw the barman crouched before the saloon's front window, inspecting the two bullet holes as if they might be repaired.

"Here's your faro cut," he said, tossing the man a small cloth pouch.

The man caught the pouch and said with a knowing grin, "What's the matter? Town gettin' too hot fer ye?"

"Reckon."

Hawk hefted his rifle in his right hand, nudged the saddlebags higher on his left shoulder, stepped off the boardwalk, and crossed the street at a southwestern angle, heading for Sanchez's Livery and Feed Barn.

Hearing hoof thuds to his left, he turned to see the town marshal and six armed, grim, fearful-looking civilians riding toward him. The small, potbellied lawman—looking no less determined than his posse—rode a tall, black horse, the man's spectacles winking in the late-day sun.

Hawk watched the six men pass, heading for the edge of town, then turned and strode through the barn's open doors.

"Lambs to the slaughter," he muttered.

In the barn's gloom, Hawk saddled his grulla mustang and strapped the wooden frame and panniers to the back of his dun packhorse. When he'd paid his stabling and feed bill, he walked the horses west up Main, past the townspeople standing in clusters and discussing the robbery. Behind him, the woman in the orange dress was sobbing on the porch of the millinery shop, two other women patting her back and offering handkerchiefs.

Hawk tied his horses to the hitching post out front of the Pagosa Springs Mercantile, then went inside and off-loaded every penny of his meager faro winnings. Less than fifteen minutes later, he came back out, stowed the coffee, sugar, flour, side-pork, beans, and ammunition in the panniers, then mounted the grulla and walked the horses out of town.

Breaking into a canter and keeping his eyes peeled on the stage road, he followed the tracks of the eight bank robbers overlaid by those of the six posse men. When he'd ridden for nearly an hour into the pine tables and red-rock scarps southwest of town, he reined up suddenly and squinted into the distance, listening.

Pistols and rifles cracked faintly. The reports seemed to originate from the base of a rocky mesa about five miles northwest.

He heeled the grulla into a gallop, soon leaving the stage road for the high, open desert stippled with firs and scored by deep, rocky ravines. At the top of a hogback, the rider reined the grulla to a skidding halt.

Below, a high-sided gully had been carved by an ancient river flowing down from Black Mountain, probably used as a buffalo jump by the Indians. It was a good place to trap men, as well. The bank robbers had taken full advantage.

Firing from the opposite ridge spotted with boulders and wind-bent pines, the gunmen had opened fire on the posse as the marshal and the townsmen had followed the robbers' trail across the ravine and up a notch in the ridge.

None of the riders had made it to the ridge's crest, however.

To a man, they all lay dead amidst the small, round stones and three downed horses at the bottom of the cut.

2.

TRACK-DOWN

HAWK didn't take time to bury the dead. Their fellow townsmen could do that.

He paused to shoot one of the horses the killers had left to drown in its own blood. Leaving his packhorse hobbled near a spring, he gigged the grulla up the ridge from which the bushwhackers had fired down on the posse. Amidst the rocks and small pines, their cartridge casings glistened in the west-falling light.

Hawk picked up the killers' trail on the north side of the ridge. He galloped off through a narrow cut between the hills, heading north into the San Juans rising before him like a ruffled velvet curtain, the high, rocky crests mantled with small glaciers.

On his way from Pagosa Springs, a hard, cold rock had grown in his stomach—an urgency to catch up to the killers before they could kill the girls. It was nearly the same urgency he'd felt when he'd ridden up the hill to save his son.

But he'd been too late to save Jubal from being hanged by "Three Fingers" Ned Meade, and Jubal's body had hung slack from the cottonwood, twisting and turning in the lashing wind and rain.

Hard-jawed, hat tipped low over his forehead, Hawk now rode with one eye on the trail ahead and one eye on the hoof-pocked ground beneath his grulla's pounding feet, throwing an occasional glance behind. He doubted the robbers knew he was fogging them. They'd be cocky and confident now that they'd hornswoggled the posse. But he didn't want to make the same mistake the townsmen had.

He paused to let his horse draw water from a run-out spring, then made his own tinhorn mistake, which cost him a good half hour of waning daylight. A mile from the spring, he realized he was following an older trail of four riders instead of eight. Cursing, he turned back to the spring, picked up the fresh eight-horse trail, and once again headed northwest into the shelving foothills over which the night was quickly descending.

Urgency gnawed at him.

The girls had been grabbed off the boardwalk before the bank for the depraved, whimsical pleasures of the bank robbers, and to taunt the town's inept law and citizens. If Hawk didn't get to the girls soon, they'd be raped and killed, probably dumped in a ravine where no one would ever find them.

As Hawk whipped the rein ends against the grulla's pounding flanks, coyotes yodeled. The small, brown figures of feeding mule deer stood along tawny, sun-gilded western slopes, their shadows long beneath them.

In the east, the evening's first star kindled. A chill, early-autumn breeze sung down from the glaciers, rife with the fragrance of pine sap and snow.

Good dark found Hawk crouched on a pine-studded ridge top, his rifle in his hands, staring into a hollow in which nestled a small ranch headquarters.

A large cook fire burned before the small, log cabin, lighting the whole yard. The robbers stood around it, eating deer meat with their hands, staggering or sitting on wooden stools, drinking from tin cups or bottles. Hawk was a good quarter mile away as the crow flies, but he could hear their jubilant whoops and hollers on the chill night wind.

He studied the yard through his field glasses. He saw nothing of the girls. They might be in the cabin. The men seemed to be making frequent trips to the cabin in turn.

Shouldering up to a large boulder and hunkered down on his right knee, Hawk lowered the field glasses and rubbed a gloved hand across his jaw. He'd donned his buckskin coat trimmed with coyote fur, and had turned the collar up.

Eight men against one. He could head straight down the slope, shooting, but he'd probably only get two or three at the most before they laid him out. That wouldn't do the girls any good at all.

He'd have to take his time, sneak around the cabin, take them by surprise. Even then, the odds weren't good. . . .

When he lowered his hand toward his rifle butt, he felt the familiar lump in his pocket. He removed his glove and reached inside, wrapped his fingers around the smooth wooden horse carved by his son, Jubal, and squeezed.

Steeled with resolve, he pulled his hand from the pocket, donned the glove, and returned the field glasses to their case. He stood, strode quickly down the slope opposite the cabin, to where he'd tethered the grulla to a pine branch, and dropped the glasses into his saddlebags. He took the rifle under his right arm, removed his silver-plated Russian .44 from his cross-draw holster, and filled the empty chamber under the hammer. Returning the Russian to its holster, he did the same thing to the stag-butted Army Colt in the holster on his right hip, and spun the cylinder.

"You stay, boy," he told the horse. "I won't be long."

Hawk snugged his hat down low on his head, hefted the rifle in his hands, and hurried down the slope behind the horse. At the bottom of the narrow, pine-choked draw through which a thin, ice-fringed stream trickled darkly, touched with starlight, he turned left and followed the stream for a good quarter mile.

Two flat pistol shots sounded from the other side

of the ridge. Hawk froze, staring unseeing at a rotten pine log on the ground to his left, listening.

A night bird cooed.

Hawk swallowed the dry knot in his throat and jogged on.

A half hour later, breathing heavily, he stepped out of the woods at the cabin's rear. He took a moment to catch his wind, then ran crouching past a leaning privy and, approaching a trash pile mounded twenty feet from the cabin's back wall, heard a tinny clatter and a sudden, snorting whimper.

He wheeled right, snapping the Henry to his shoulder and sighting down the barrel. Just as quickly, he eased the tension in his trigger finger and lowered the rifle back down to his side as the coyote clattered over the empty tins, away from Hawk, and disappeared into the brush at the opposite side of the yard.

Hawk let out a relieved breath.

He turned and strode to the cabin's back wall and crept to the left rear corner, eased a look around the side, toward the front yard. A lean-to roof angled down the cabin's east side, merely a rickety shelter for firewood stacked against the wall. A few rusty washtubs hulked in the darkness, leaning against the wood. Hanging from the posts supporting the roof were several steel animal traps.

Beyond the lean-to, out front of the cabin, Hawk could see part of the fire reaching seven feet high, sending sparks and smoke buffeting skyward. Sap bubbles popped frequently, showering the ground with glowing embers, evoking occasional curses from the revelers.

Somewhere out of Hawk's field of vision, one of the robbers was strumming a jubilant guitar tune and singing. Another sang along, hooting moronically and, from the sound of it, dancing a scuffling sort of jig while clutching a sloshing liquor bottle. Several others were reenacting the robbery, while another was talking about the whore he planned to see next week in Denver City.

Behind a lantern-lit window, which the woodpile had been stacked around, Hawk could hear other voices inside and the soft snaps of cards being flipped onto a table.

Lifting the Henry with his right hand, Hawk wrapped his left hand around the barrel, adjusting his deerskin-gloved fingers on the smooth iron, and stepped forward around the woodpile. He crouched low to pass before the window.

Seeing two human figures out of the corner of his right eye, he stopped suddenly with an involuntary grunt, and stepped back. He turned his head toward the woodpile.

His stomach lurched.

Directly beneath the window, the stove-length cordwood had been stacked only bench-high. On it the two girls sat, slouched back against the cabin wall, on either side of the window. They were both naked, blood-smeared, and pale. They could have been sleeping, but bullets had been drilled through the foreheads of each.

Their delicate hands rested in their laps. Their slender legs and feet, impossibly white and fragile, hung down toward the ground, dangling there against the logs.

Hawk stared, eyes slitted, wringing the rifle in his hands.

He remembered how his wife had looked after he'd taken her down from the tree from which she'd hanged herself the morning after Jubal was murdered, when the townswomen had removed her clothes and laid her out upon the kitchen table to wash her for burial. . . .

Pale. Delicate. A shell of blood and bones.

Hawk swallowed now and stepped up to the window.

He stared between the heads of the two girls, through the dusty glass, into the cabin. Three men lounged around a wooden table, in the cluttered front room, the log walls papered with the yellow pages of old, illustrated newspapers. The men were playing poker.

One—the lanky kid with long pewter hair and pewter chin whiskers—lounged back in his chair, ankles crossed on the table, facing the window. He was laughing, stretching his lips back from the long, black cigar clamped between his teeth, at the man sitting to his left, sideways to the window.

The man was shaking his head and rubbing his temple with his left finger as he studied the cards fanned in his hand. The man across the table from him plucked a silver cartwheel from a large pile of coins beside his left elbow, and tossed it into the pot. This man—a stocky, blond gent with a red beard and fresh cuts on both cheekbones in the half-moon shapes of fingernails—wore a torn gingham frock around his shoulders, capelike.

"Whoo-eee, Brent," said the young man with the pewter hair, "you're reachin' pretty deep in that new poke o' yourn!"

Jaws clamped hard with rage, Hawk took one more step toward the window, turned his rifle barrel toward him, and rammed the butt against the glass, which broke apart like a fragile puzzle. The clinking, clattering din was drowned out as Hawk swung the rifle barrel forward, poked it through the window, aimed at the stocky man with the cape, and fired.

The man hadn't hit the floor, before Hawk, jacking a fresh round in the chamber, deftly swung the rifle toward the kid with the pewter hair, and squeezed the trigger. The kid's startled eyes had just found Hawk's when the .44-round blew the kid's Adam's apple out the back of his neck.

The third man swung toward the window, standing and reaching for the pistol on his right hip. Hawk aimed quickly but precisely, and drilled a neat, round hole through the man's broad, sunburned forehead, in roughly the same place the girls had been shot.

Hawk didn't wait to see the man turn a bizarre pirouette on his way to the floor. He pulled the rifle from the window and, hearing the shocked, angry yells from the front of the cabin, retraced his steps to the cabin's back wall.

Striding smoothly, holding his cocked rifle
straight up and down before his chest, he raked a
glance around the opposite corner, toward the fire's
glow at the front. Shouts and running footsteps rose
from the lean-to as Hawk slipped around the corner
and dashed toward the front of the cabin. He didn't
pause near the corner. He trotted around it, stopped in
the front yard between the stoop and the crackling
bonfire, dropped to a knee, and raised the Winchester to his shoulder.

As three figures appeared at the opposite corner,
running back around the cabin from the lean-to,
Hawk snugged his cheek against the rifle's walnut
stock, picked out one of the bright-eyed silhouettes,
and fired.

At the same time, the first man stopped and raised
the pistol in his right hand, yelling, "There!"

The exclamation came out as a grunt as Hawk's
.44 slug plowed through his chest, halfway between
his heart and his throat, and sent him tumbling back
into the man to his left.

The collision nudged the second man's arm, so
that the shot the man squeezed off slammed into the
ground a good six feet to Hawk's left. Calmly but
quickly, Hawk ejected his spent shell, which arced
back over his right shoulder as he rammed a fresh
one into the chamber, and squeezed the trigger.

The second man was still stumbling back and
sideways. Hawk's slug merely blew the straw sombrero from his head and evoked an exasperated Spanish curse.

Again, Hawk levered the rifle and fired. This bullet pounded the man's upper left chest, throwing him into a sort of off-shoulder roll.

Hearing shouts and running feet behind him, Hawk triggered another pill at the tall, skinny man who'd rounded the corner with the other two. Crouching, feet spread wide, the man was edging toward the fire, two big Colts extended in his bony hands.

The man dodged back to his own right, and Hawk's slug missed its mark.

The running men were nearly on Hawk now. Not having time for another shot, Hawk threw himself left and down, hitting the ground on his right shoulder and throwing himself head-first into the cabin. The tall man's Colts roared, tearing gobbets out of the stoop's floor and the cabin's log walls.

"Hold it, boys—it's me!" the tall man shouted.

Too late. The running men rounded the cabin corner, furiously triggering lead. The tall man yelped. Hawk leapt toward the bracket lamp beside the door. In the corner of his right eye, Hawk saw the tall man drop to a knee, clutching his right wrist and screeching like a rooster getting its neck wrung.

An angry voice shouted, cracking with fury, "Where the fuck is he?"

"In there!" shrieked the big man.

Pressing a shoulder against the front wall, Hawk heard the men running toward him. "Get out here, you son of a bitch!"

3.

ZAMACONA

HAWK listened to the men's boots pounding toward the cabin. When he figured they were only about ten feet from the stoop, he cocked his Henry.

They wanted him, they'd have him.

Hawk stepped into the doorway.

The men stopped abruptly, rifles in their hands but not aimed at the door. The savage fury in their eyes changed to shock. They'd thought they were going to have to root him out of the cabin.

Hawk brought his rifle to bear on the man on the left. As the man's mouth opened, Hawk shot him, clipping his scream. As the other man swung the barrel of his rifle toward the doorway, Hawk shot him, too.

Both dropped like fresh cow plops, the first one

dead before he'd hit the ground, the other moving as if to lift himself onto his hands and knees.

A shot sounded to Hawk's left, the slug plunking into the awning support post before him. Hawk bolted off the porch, fired at the skinny man kneeling near the fire, a pistol extended in his left hand. As the man cursed and fired again, the slug nicking the post and plunking into the cabin wall behind Hawk, Hawk's second shot hit home.

As the skinny man dropped, Hawk turned his gaze to the packed yard before the cabin. The man who'd tried to gain his hands and knees had rolled onto his right shoulder, hat lying on the ground beneath him. Weakly, he raised a Schofield revolver in his shaking right hand, squinting his eyes at Hawk. His face was drawn and haggard behind his full dragoon mustache.

"You b-bastard." The pistol was too much for him. He dropped it. "Who the hell are you, anyway?"

Hawk took his rifle in his left hand and inched the right lapels of both coats back from his chest, revealing the moon-and-star marshal's badge pinned to his shirt.

The man's left eye slitted. *"Lawman?"*

"That's right."

The man was incredulous. "You never . . . never even gave us a chance. Ain't you supposed to give us a chance?"

"After what you did to that town, that posse, and to those two girls . . ."

The man's chest rose and fell sharply. "But that's the law!"

"Not my law," Hawk said. As he took his rifle in his right hand and aimed at the man's head, the man's eyes snapped wide.

"No!"

The man's plea was punctuated by the explosion of Hawk's Henry. As the slug tore through it, basting the short, tough grass and gravel with bone, brains, and blood, the man's head bounced off the ground, then fell back again and lay still.

Hawk looked around. The tall man was the only one now moving. He had two bullets in his hide, but it must've been a tough hide. He was up on all fours, crawling away from the fire.

Levering another shell into his sixteen-shot Henry's breech, Hawk walked over to the man, lifted his left boot, and planted it down hard on the man's back.

The outlaw collapsed with a shrill scream.

Holding him down with his foot, Hawk snugged his rifle's barrel against the back of the man's head, and pulled the trigger. When the echo of the shot had died, he heard a leathery squeak and looked up sharply.

Thirty feet away, a man sat a horse.

The newcomer was mostly concealed by the darkness beyond the fire, but Hawk saw a low-crowned sombrero, calico shirt, and a red sash. The horse's neck owned an Arabian arch. Chihuahua spurs with three-inch needle rowels flashed in the firelight. The man gripped his reins with both hands, holding both up close to his chest, as if to show he was not wielding a weapon.

"No need to shoot, Señor. I am your friend from the saloon."

The man gigged his horse slowly forward. He stopped ten feet from Hawk, and offered a caballero-like bow of his head. "Toribio Zamacona."

He was, indeed, the Mexican piano player and lip-smacking tequila drinker from the saloon. When Zamacona reached into the breast pocket of his calico shirt, Hawk loudly rammed another shell and raised the Henry.

The man stopped.

His broad lips pulled back from even, white teeth. Slowly, with only his thumb and index finger, he reached into the pocket, removed a quarter-folded paper, snapped it open, and held it out to his side. "Four of these men are wanted, Señor. I recognized them when they first rode into town."

Hawk glanced at the paper in which the likenesses of four men had been sketched below REWARD in large, block letters. He looked at Zamacona. "A piano-playin' bounty hunter?"

The Mexican's smile broadened. "Sí."

"You look like a vaquero."

"Bounty hunters who look like bounty hunters live on short strings."

"What the hell took you so long to get here?"

Zamacona lifted a shoulder and canted his head sheepishly. "Inebriated bounty hunters don't live long, either. I had a nap. After so much tequila, I could have done little to help the *gringas*."

"Yeah, well . . . I couldn't do it, either," Hawk growled.

The Mexican glanced at the dead men strewn about the yard, partly shadowed shapes upon which the umber firelight played. He turned his head to Hawk, a faint admiration in his eyes. "Nice work, Señor."

He opened his fingers, releasing the wanted dodger, which fluttered down to the ground, hanging up on a buckbrush clump. "The reward is yours. Farewell." He neck-reined the Arab sharply right.

"Hold on," Hawk said, lowering his rifle barrel.

The man turned back to him.

"If you help me get those girls back to their families, the reward money's yours."

The Mexican arched his black brows skeptically. "Señor?"

"I have no use for blood money. Only blood."

Smelling the gore around the cabin, the Arab fiddle-footed. The man held the reins tight in his fists, kept his thighs squeezed against the saddle. He chuckled.

"What man could refuse such an offer?"

There were nearly a dozen horses in the main corral of the outlaw ranch. Hawk and Zamacona bridled nine, one for each dead outlaw and one for the two dead girls.

When the blanket-wrapped bodies were tied over the horses' backs, Hawk led the grisly procession back toward town, crossing the wash in which the dead posse lay ghostly pale in the moonlight. When Hawk had retrieved his packhorse, he popped off a couple shots at the coyotes milling around the wash.

When he holstered his pistol and continued riding, he heard the Mexican, riding at the end of the line, mutter a prayer. The dead men's relatives would no doubt retrieve the bodies the next day—what was left of them. Hawk didn't have enough horses to do so himself, and rounding up the posse's mounts would have been impossible in the darkness.

An hour later, Hawk topped a low ridge. Below, the town was a black mass of lumpy, dark shapes in the valley bottom. A few lantern-lit windows shown like sparse fireflies. Bats flapped against the stars.

Hawk stepped down, freed his packhorse from the string, then mounted his grulla and, trailing only the dun, rode back to Zamacona. He stuck out his hand. "They're all yours, amigo."

The Mexican's voice betrayed his befuddlement. "Where are you going, Señor? It is late. . . ."

"Worn out my stay around here. Time to move on."

Zamacona sighed. "I suppose it does not take long for an outlaw lawman to wear out his stay anywhere."

Hawk leveled a quizzical look at him.

The Mexican lifted his left hand palm-up. "Who else could you be but *el mariscal del asesino*? Only a zealous killer could have taken down all these *banditos*. A man who does not fear death, uh?" He spit chew to one side. "Travel with caution, Señor Hawk. Your reputation as the killing marshal precedes you. Even in Mejico."

"Last I heard there was a reward on my head," Hawk said, keeping his hand near his holster. "Fifteen hundred dollars."

"I could live a long time on so much money." The man flashed a white-toothed smile. "But I do not tangle with men who care little if they live or die."

He held out his right hand. Hawk shook it, pinched his hat brim, and reined his horse northward as Zamacona took the reins of the lead horse and headed down into Pagosa Springs.

Steering by the North Star, Hawk followed wagon traces and horse trails into the foothills of the San Juan Mountains looming ahead like a black theater curtain. He gained the Del Norte mining road about an hour before dawn, and traced its winding course into the mountains' bulging aprons and deep canyons, gradually climbing toward the high parks where the air smelled stony and damp and scented with pine resin.

From a far peak, between breezes, he heard the occasional, eerie cries of a mountain lion.

At ten o'clock the next morning, he followed the faint trail between two enormous pines, and stopped.

Beyond and right, a small, sun-dappled clearing opened, spotted here and there with dirty snowdrifts from an early autumn squall. Hawk's cabin sat back in the pines, flanked by a stream meandering along the base of a high, forested ridge. It was a low, square hovel of hand-adzed logs, with a shake roof and a tin stovepipe. Moss spotted the shakes, as the cabin was shaded by the trees and the mountain most of the day.

A small stable and pole corral stood to the right. Against the cabin's east wall, Hawk had stacked firewood, and he added to it every chance he got.

He'd found the cabin abandoned in the early spring. Asking around the small mining camp a mile down the mountain, he'd found that the miner who'd lived here had died from a tooth infection that had spread into his brain.

Hawk had moved in, made some minor repairs to the old shack, replacing shakes and adding a narrow front stoop. He'd spent the summer here unmolested, and he intended to spend the winter here, as well. In the spring, he'd move on. The neighboring miners had already grown curious about the man who'd moved into the prospector's shack but did no prospecting.

A wanted man—especially a wanted lawman—couldn't let the grass grow too long under his boots. The Mexican had been wrong. Hawk wanted to live long enough to kill a hundred men who deserved it. Only then, he believed, could he feel another moment's peace, another moment free of fury, before he died.

But for the rest of the fall and winter, he wanted some peace and quiet. Time for the fervor around his reputation to die down, so he could head out of the mountains and track killers again without having to keep such a sharp eye on his own backtrail.

Hawk sat the grulla at the edge of the clearing, scrutinizing the cabin, always wary of an ambush. He'd been on the run from lawmen and bounty hunters for the past year, after seven years as a bona fide marshal himself. He'd learned to step lightly and to take no chances.

He sat there long enough for anyone watching from the cabin to get a good look at him. Then, dropping the dun's reins, he turned the grulla 180 degrees, headed back the way he'd come for twenty yards, then turned sharply into the forest. He kept the horse moving swiftly, ducking under branches, gripping the horn as the mustang leapt shrubs and deadfalls.

Hoping to catch any possible ambushers off guard, he burst from the forest ten minutes later and splashed across the swift-flowing creek. He gripped his Russian in his right hand, the Colt in his left, as he galloped up to the cabin's rear wall, raking his cautious gaze this way and that. Seeing no one lurking around the back, he cantered a complete circle around the structure, then circled the stable and corral.

Finally, he raced the horse back to the cabin, dismounted, leapt the steps to the porch, and turned an ear to the timbered door. Silence. He turned his key in the lock. Holding both cocked pistols straight out before him, he shoved the door wide.

In the shadows, a screech sounded.

He snapped his guns to the left and down toward the floor. His eyes still adjusting from the high-country light, he glimpsed a gray-brown blur as a mouse slipped through a knot in the puncheon floor, beneath Hawk's small eating table.

Hawk lowered his guns, depressing his hammers. "Reckon I'm gonna have to get a cat."

When he'd decided he was alone here, he retrieved the packhorse and began setting his stores in order. For the next three days, he cleaned the cabin, hauled and split wood, and hunted, filling his outdoor cellar with fresh venison and hanging jerky to dry on a rope strung before his sheet-iron stove.

He was sitting before the stove three nights later, reading a Shakespeare play the cabin's original owner had left behind, as a light rain pelted his low, sashed windows. Hooves thudded outside, splashing through the mud. In the corral, his own horses whinnied a warning.

Hawk had exchanged the book in his hand for his silver-plated Russian, when a light tap sounded on his door. Hawk thumbed the hammer back.

4.

CATHERINE MCCORMICK

THE girl's voice was barely audible above the rain and the lashing wind. "Mr. Hollis?"

George Hollis was Hawk's alias.

Hawk remained in his elk-horn rocker. He'd locked the shutters over the cabin's three windows, so the only danger would come from the door.

"Come in."

The door opened slowly. A pretty, oval face, framed in long, dark brown hair and a hooded black cape, pushed through the opening. The young woman's eyes flickered fearfully when they saw the gun. Hawk kept it leveled.

"Miss McCormick?" Her family was one of the dozen or so from the mining camp on the other side of the mountain. When Hawk shot more meat than he needed, he often hauled the extra down to the camp in return for canned goods or the miners' dark, home-brewed ale.

She had a Scottish accent to go along with those high, chiseled cheekbones, obsidian eyes, and long, dark hair, several damp strands of which fell from the cape's hood. "I saw your horse on the ridge the other day."

Hawk depressed his Colt's hammer, stood, and crossed the small room to the door in three strides. He pulled the door wide, peered into the night behind the girl. Seeing only a steeldust mare tethered to the hitch rack before his dripping stoop, he said, "Come in." He closed the door behind her.

"Sorry to interrupt."

"You're not interrupting anything, Miss Mc-Cormick. What brings you up here in this weather, this time of the night?"

Catherine McCormick reached up with both her gloved hands and lowered the hood, shook out her hair. Hawk didn't know how old she was. He guessed eighteen or nineteen. Her smooth-skinned face was pale, her tear-glazed eyes creased with sorrow.

"Last week, during the snowstorm, evil men came to the camp and savaged the girls." She pursed her lips, trying to stifle her emotions, but tears rolled down her cheeks. "They stayed all night and killed five men . . . including my brother, Liam."

Hawk dragged a chair out from his eating table. He wasn't sure how this involved him—unless she knew who he really was. "Sit down."

She sat. Hawk reached into a peach crate he'd

nailed up for a shelf, extracted a flat bottle. He
popped the cork, splashed the brandy into a tin cup,
set it before the girl. "Drink up. It'll make you feel
better."

"Nothing's going to make me feel better, Mr. Hollis. They shot my only brother. My mother is bedrid-
den with sorrow. My father and the other men tried
tracking the killers. . . ." She touched the cup to her
lips, made a face.

"Were you . . . ?"

Catherine McCormick shook her head. "Pa hid me
in our cellar."

Hawk took a hide-bottom chair across from the
girl. "How many in the group?"

"Ten, fifteen, maybe more. There was a woman
with them, dressed like a man. They were Ameri-
cans, but Pa heard them say they'd come up from
Mexico. They'd been hiding out down there for the
past two years, and this was their first trip back."

Anger pinched the girl's rich, pink lips. "They
were celebrating, I guess. Raping and killing. Having
a grand time." She ran her right palm across her face,
bringing a flush to her cheeks. "And my brother, only
ten years old, lies dead in his grave."

Hawk didn't say anything.

"How can it be, Mr. Hawk?" She was staring at
him, as if she expected an answer. "How can something like this happen? We did nothing to provoke
those—"

She stopped, her eyes snapping wide as she realized that she'd slipped and called him by his real

name. Hawk stared at her, lines forming in the bridge
of his nose. Slowly, she stuck a hand into a pocket of
the cape, brought out a small, thin book with a yellow cover.

The cover had been turned back, the book folded
lengthwise. Folding it open, she set the book on the
table.

Hawk looked at it. *The Tale of the Rogue Lawman*
was the story's main title. In small letters below the
title was written: "How a Respected Western Lawman Turned to Bloody Murder!"

Hawk leaned back in his chair.

"Addicted to the illustrated storybooks, I'm
afraid," said the girl, chagrined.

Hawk grabbed the brandy bottle from the table,
stood, and walked to the peach crate. Another cup sat
on the shelf, a half-smoked cigar residing within. He
removed the half-smoked cigar, blew out the dust
and ashes, and poured brandy into the cup.

Thoughtfully facing the carved horse and a tintype
picture of him and his wife and child, both of which
he'd propped against the scarred logs, he threw back
the liquor.

"Does your father know you're here?"

"No."

"You want me to hunt those men. . . ."

"I can't pay you anything, Mr. Hawk." He heard
her chair slide back from the table, the rustle of her
clothes as she stood. For a moment, she said nothing.
"But I can stay with you tonight."

Hawk turned. The girl stood on the other side of

the table, her cape lowered to her waist. She hadn't
been wearing anything beneath it. Naked from the
waist up, she stood before him, eyes lowered demurely. Her breasts were surprisingly full for a girl
so slight. Gooseflesh stood out on her skin.

Hawk set his cup on the table and moved to the
girl. He looked down at her pale shoulders, her thick,
damp hair falling over them. The breasts were full,
with large areolas and jutting, brown nipples. Her
head was lowered, her chest rising and falling
sharply. Beneath his gaze, more gooseflesh rose on
her skin.

Hawk felt nothing but a steely determination to
kill. The feeling—or lack of feeling—would have
frightened most men. Hawk had cultivated it.

Slowly, Hawk lifted the cape over those fragile
shoulders, covering the breasts. She looked up at
him, tiny lines spoking her eyes, questioning.

"You're beautiful." Hawk placed his hands on her
neck and spread them apart, lifting the hair out from
beneath her cape. "I don't take payment for hunting
killers. You go on home and rest assured the men
who killed your brother will die."

She gazed up at him through narrowed eyes. Her
mouth opened several times uncertainly. Finally, she
looked away. "Thank you, Mr. Hawk."

As she moved slowly, reluctantly toward the door,
Hawk said, "Does anyone else in the camp know
who I am?"

She stopped, one hand on the doorknob, and
shook her head.

"I'd be obliged if you kept it that way."

She turned to him hopefully. "Will you be back?"

"Doubtful. But the fewer people who know who I am, the better."

She pinched her lips together with disappointment, opened the door, glanced back at him once more, then closed the door behind her. In a moment, Hawk heard her horse's hooves making wet, sucking sounds as it slogged slowly off through the rain.

At roughly the same time of the night but on the other side of the Colorado Territory, an enclosed black carriage splashed along the stage road west of Trinidad.

Rain knifed down from the gauzy-dark sky. Lightning forked. Thunder cracked and rumbled. Rain sluiced through the road's deep ruts, making the trail a virtual river.

Glancing out the coach's hide-draped window, the territorial governor of Colorado, John L. Routt, cursed silently. Goddamn Gideon Hawk for making his life so miserable, for dragging Routt away from Denver on a night like this. The Rogue Lawman, as he'd become known in law enforcement circles, had been a bee in Routt's bonnet for over a year. Tonight, however, would be the beginning of the end. . . .

Routt let the curtain fall closed, shutting out the rain, and leaned back in his seat with a weary sigh, chewing his mustache.

The team slowed as it rounded a long bend, splashing through a swirling wash. Routt again peeked through the curtain. The carriage rolled to a halt before a two-story stage station and roadhouse whose lantern-lit windows offered the only light between the storm's blue flashes.

Three other carriages were parked before the building's broad front porch, long tongues drooping in the mud, their teams no doubt enjoying the fresh hay in the barn on the other side of the road.

"Finally, we're here," Routt said to the carriage's only other passenger as he plucked his beaver hat off the opposite seat and set it carefully upon his balding head.

The coach jostled as the driver and the shotgun rider hustled down from the driver's box. As the shotgun rider swung the coach door wide, Routt stepped out and raised the fox-fur collar of his long, wool coat. With a gloved hand, he snugged his beaver hat down low on his forehead, as if the nearly nonexistent brim could shield his steel-rimmed spectacles from the rain.

Behind him, the other passenger—a taller, younger man than Routt—stepped down from the coach and adjusted the brace of pistols positioned butt-forward on his lean hips, then pulled his sheepskin coat down over the pearl handles. He snugged his broad-brimmed black hat low on his freckled forehead, flung his long, red hair out from under his collar, looked around, and followed the older man toward the building.

"Mr. Governor!" the driver yelled as he walked

out from behind the coach, wincing against the weather.

Routt turned, using a gloved index finger to hold his glasses firmly against the bridge of his nose. His long mustaches and spade beard rippled in the wind.

"I didn't know we was in for this much of a gully-washer. Reckon we oughta spend the night here, instead of headin' back to Trinny-dad?"

Bowing his head against the wind and rain, the governor cast the station a wary glance.

"Ole Stanley's got the place well stocked with girls." The driver grinned.

Routt slid his eyes to the taller, younger man beside him. It was a snide, silent exchange. The governor held out his free hand as if to indicate the weather. "I guess we don't have much choice. But don't get too inebriated, Dexter. I need to be at the train station by noon."

He started toward the cabin, stopped, and turned back to the driver. "And remember, Mr. Dexter, you're a married man!"

"Thanks for reminding me, sir!" Chuckling, the driver looked at the shotgun messenger, who'd turned to begin unhitching the team. "That's a tragic little fact I just can't seem to keep fixed in my noggin!"

Lightning flashed and thunder roared like crashing boulders as Routt, flanked by the red-haired man, crossed the porch and entered the main cabin. He took two steps inside the front door and paused, removing his rain-splattered hat and glasses. His near-

sighted eyes made out three well-dressed dudes—
the assistants of the men he'd come here to meet—
gathered around one table to his left. They didn't
look happy to be there. Nevertheless, they all waved
or nodded at Routt.

At another table, playing poker and smoking,
were a handful of crusty sorts in battered hats and
sombreros, wet jackets drying before a crackling fire:
the drivers of the other carriages.

A short, stocky figure moved toward Routt, limping as deep as an arthritic old woman. Swarthy and
black-mustachioed, the man was clad in brushed
broadcloth and a long, silk duster to which a five-
pointed sheriff's badge was pinned. He spoke in a
faint Mexican accent.

"Governor Routt, I'm Sheriff Ramirez. I received
your telegram and cleared the place out for you and
the other governors."

Shaking the sheriff's hand, Governor Routt said,
"Anyone but the men in this room know about this?"

"No, sir. Our lips are sealed. You chose a good
place. Since the railroad came, there are only two
stages a week through here. It's just a watering hole
for area drovers and freighters, mostly. It's pretty
quiet through the week."

Running a handkerchief over his glasses, Routt in-
troduced Ramirez to the young, redheaded man beside him. When the two had shaken hands, Ramirez
turned to Routt. "The others are waiting for you upstairs, sir."

"Lead the way."

As they crossed the room, Routt saw three men
with rain slickers and deputy's badges standing sideways to the bar running along the room's right wall.
Another, wearing an apron, stood on the other side of
the bar, playing a desultory game of checkers with
the man facing him. A rifle lay across the bar's
planks. Several more old-model Winchesters leaned
against the whiskey kegs at each end of the bar. The
deputies cast the governor vaguely snide glances,
then, unimpressed—irked, in fact, to have been
dragged out in such weather—went back to their
game and bored conversations.

Routt and the red-haired gent followed the sheriff
up the staircase at the back of the room. As the three
walked along a narrow, second-story hall lit by two
smoking bracket lamps, Routt stopped before a
closed door with chipped green paint and two shaggy
bullet holes. Behind the door, bedsprings squawked,
and a woman groaned with practiced melodrama.

Chuckling with embarrassment, the sheriff turned
and limped back toward Routt. "One of my deputies
is enjoying the attentions of one of the *putas*. They're
quite famous around here, you know. The boy
doesn't get out much. I saw no harm."

On the other side of the hall, a doorknob clicked.
Routt turned as another door opened. A young, dark-
skinned woman with short, kinky black hair stood in
the doorway. She was dressed in a short, sheer, powder-
blue wrapper that revealed nearly all of her cherry-
chocolate thighs. She ran her suggestive gaze down
the governor's paunchy but otherwise solid frame.

"Hello there," she purred, offering a sultry smile as she leaned against the door frame and let the wrapper drop low, revealing nearly all of one nubbin breast. "My, aren't we bein' visited by important-looking gents this evenin'."

"An octoroon," the governor said, arching a brow with interest.

"You can call me Maggie," said the girl. One bare foot perched upon the other, she wagged a bare knee.

The red-haired gent cleared his throat. "Remember, sir, you're married."

The governor winced, as though he'd been elbowed sharply in the ribs. Running his gaze down the girl's wrapper, he grumbled, "I've always been partial to octoroons."

"I've always been partial to important men," said the girl.

"You'll be here all evening?" Routt asked her.

The girl rested her head against the door frame. "In weather like this, where would I go?"

"Perhaps I'll see you later."

"Perhaps I'll be right here." Backing into the room and holding the governor's gaze with her own, she closed the door, latching it softly.

The sheriff chuckled and winked at the governor. "You won't be sorry with Maggie, sir."

"I've always been partial to octoroons," Routt said to the red-haired gent as they both continued following the sheriff toward a closed door at the far end of the hall.

5.

DEATH WARRANT

RAMIREZ walked into the room at the end of the hall, then stepped aside as Governor Routt and the red-haired gent entered behind him.

The room was small, furnished with only a shabby fainting couch and a large, round table over which a stained-glass lamp hung from the ceiling. Around the table sat three middle-aged, well-dressed men, leaning back in their chairs, looking bored.

A bottle sat on the table, and before each man was a cut-glass decanter and ashtray. All but one smoked a cigar. The smoke hung so thick in the room that the men's features were blurred.

"Sorry to keep you waiting, gentlemen," Routt said, unbuttoning his long coat. "The train was late, and this weather . . ."

"Hello, John," greeted the oldest of the three, tipping his gray head back to blow smoke at the ceiling. He chuckled as if at a joke obvious to them all.

"John, what in blue blazes are we doing here?" said a man with a full, brown beard. Sam Axtell, governor of New Mexico Territory, wore a brown foulard tie against a paper collar. Gold, square-framed spectacles perched high on his nose.

The territorial governor of Arizona sat with his back to the door. A.P.K. "Anson" Safford turned in his chair to regard Routt haughtily. "Do you have any idea what a grand time the press would have if they knew that four territorial governors were meeting in a *brothel*?"

"Come, now, gentlemen—don't tell me you've never visited a brothel before."

Puffing smoke, the oldest governor—George W. Emery of Utah—chuckled, blue eyes twinkling. "Oh, I've visited plenty of brothels in my day, John, but not one this far out in the tall and uncut. I did notice a spry little half-breed as I was climbing the stairs, however. Since it looks as though we'll be spending the evening, I call dibs on her."

"Act your age and not your shoe size, George," Safford admonished. He was the youngest governor in the room, and by far the most high-strung.

"She's all yours, George," Routt said. "When I summoned you all here, I didn't know the station had become a brothel, but I reckon I'll partake of the place's finery myself. I saw downstairs you'd all brought your assistants. They and your drivers have been sworn to secrecy, I take it?"

"Of course," said Axtell. "Now, how about you telling us just what it is exactly—aside from the girls—they're supposed to be keeping a secret."

Routt had removed his coat and thrown it over a chair. Ramirez had already left the room, but the tall, red-haired gent with the twin revolvers stood in the shadows near the door.

Routt spoke with the man quietly. The man nodded and sat in the straight-back chair left of the door. He set his black hat on his knee, crossed his boots beneath his chair.

Routt tossed his hat onto the fainting couch, where the other men had tossed theirs. He moved to the table, sat down in the fourth chair, splashed brandy into a goblet, and took a long drink.

He set his glass on the table. "We have a federal lawman who needs removal, gentlemen. I believe we all know who I'm talking about."

"Hawk!" Emery spit with a bemused smile. "Sure as the pony drip I'm liable to contract this very evening."

"I know from the papers that the marshal—ex-marshal, I should say—has been as big a thorn in your sides as he's been in mine," said Routt. "He continues to hunt outlaws as a lawman, though he's nothing more than a vigilante."

Axtell snorted. "Kills 'em all, gives them no chance. Ten witnesses have sworn affidavits in New Mexico alone."

"Killing off all the cold-blooded killers ain't good for our reputations," Emery said with sarcasm. "He keeps on, we ain't gonna need *real* lawmen anymore."

Routt turned to the older governor haughtily. "George, at one time Gideon Hawk was one of the best deputy U.S. marshals in the West. But he's become an outlaw, little better than Quantrell or Bloody Bill Anderson. He's only impersonating a lawman. The fact that he's taking down law*breakers* ahead of bona fide law *officers* is a travesty of justice—even frontier justice—and you know it!"

"Ah, hell," Emery said, leaning forward and resting his forearms on the table. "I know that. Just feel sorry for the man, that's all. He lost his family, for Chrissakes." He tossed back his drink and poured another.

Anson Safford and Sam Axtell all stared at their goblets. Safford twirled the stem of his glass with his fingers. "We've all issued warrants on him, placed bounties on his head. . . ."

"I've even sent the Army out after him," said Axtell.

"What more can we do?" asked Emery.

"Issue a death warrant." Routt sipped his drink and ran a pale hand across his mustache. "Send out a man capable of tracking him down and *taking* him down."

Safford's light-brown brows met above his nose. "You mean, *kill* him?"

Routt looked at him sharply. "Can you imagine trying an ex-lawman for killing cold-blooded killers?"

"Especially those that have eluded the regular law . . ." Emery said, bemusedly knocking ash from his cigar.

"The papers and the public would have a field day at our expense," Axtell said. Wincing, he took a long drink from his glass.

Safford sighed and sat up in his chair. "God help me, I'm convinced about the need to kill this man, but I've seen nothing to convince me it can be done. Hawk has gone up against some of the most savage men on the frontier, and they're all pushing up daisies."

"But if we had a man who knows how he thinks and works," said Routt. "A man whom Hawk himself trained. A man whom Hawk once trusted like a brother and considered a friend."

The others stared at him blankly through webs of rising cigar smoke.

The Colorado governor hooked an arm on his chair back and glanced at the tall young man sitting by the door. The man stood slowly and walked toward the table, the lamplight revealing deep-set eyes, a lightly freckled face, and a mustache and goatee the same red as his long, wavy hair.

"Gentlemen," Routt said, "meet Deputy U.S. Marshal Luke Morgan."

Two weeks later, combing the Four Corners region for tips about Gideon Hawk, reported to have been seen in the area, Deputy Luke Morgan pushed out the batwings of a cantina in Del Norte, Colorado Territory.

He stood before the swinging doors and absently refolded the photograph he'd just shown the cantina's owner. The man hadn't recognized Hawk. At least, he'd said he hadn't. It was hard to tell. If the newspaper columnists were any indication, a good portion of the frontier population wanted the man they'd started calling the "Rogue Lawman" to be left to his own devices.

They didn't seem to care that Hawk was breaking the very laws he'd been sworn to uphold.

Shoving the photograph into his shirt pocket, Morgan turned his gaze to his right up the sun-washed street, past a hay cart and several milling chickens.

He froze.

A tall, dark-haired man rode toward the cantina, on a long-legged dun stallion. He wore a black frock over a wine-red vest, and a flat-brimmed black hat. He rode slowly through the shade on the other side of the street, breeze-blown hay and dust from a passing ranch wagon drifting around him, obscuring his features.

"I'll be damned," Morgan muttered.

Hawk.

Morgan's heart thudded. He slapped the Army Colt positioned for the cross-draw on his left hip. The shade slipped back from the oncoming rider. It was as if he'd surfaced from a murky lake. The mid-afternoon sun showed the two-day stubble, faintly

pocked, gaunt cheeks, and brown eyes closely abut-
ting a wide, broad nose, red and scaled from the sun
and wind.

"Take it easy, amigo," the man said to Morgan in
a nasal voice and faint Mexican accent. He held his
right hand up, palm out, far above the old-model
Remington worn high on his right hip. He grinned,
revealing two front teeth spaced a good half inch
apart. "Last time I checked, I wasn't wanted by the
law." He reined his horse to a stop at the hitch rack,
beside Morgan's own claybank. "At least, not on this
side of the border."

Morgan held the man's stare but felt his shoulders
loosen.

Chuckling, the man dismounted, lazily looped his
reins over the hitch rack, and mounted the boardwalk. Morgan stepped aside to let the rider pass. The
man regarded him with another snide grin, then disappeared into the saloon.

Morgan stood stiffly for several seconds, letting
his heartbeat slow. His pale, freckled face was
flushed with embarrassment. He turned, saw a vacant
loafer's bench right of the door, and sagged into it.

If he was going to get this flustered over a man
who merely looked like Hawk from a distance, what
was he going to do when he met up with the man
himself? Fear was only a small part of the problem.

He wondered how he was going to kill a man
who'd once been like an older brother to him. A man
who'd taught him everything he knew about tracking
and hunting men.

Hell, Morgan still dressed much like Hawk himself dressed. Morgan even wore his guns in the same position as Hawk, and had for several years kept his eyes peeled for a silver-plated Russian like the one Hawk wore in the cross-draw holster high on his left hip.

Hawk's wife, Linda, had been like a sister to Morgan. Hawk's young son, Jubal, like a nephew. How many nights had Morgan taken supper with Hawk's family and later roughhoused with the boy on their living room floor?

Morgan removed his black hat from his head, ran a gloved hand through his wavy red hair.

Damn.

But Gideon had to be taken down. He was a feral dog running loose in a chicken yard. In his right mind, Hawk himself would agree. When the time came, Morgan would drop the hammer on his friend and mentor.

Firm in his resolve, young Morgan set his crisp hat on his head, stood, and crossed the boardwalk. Only half-hearing the clatter of the roulette wheel and the giggling whores inside the cantina, he untied his reins from the hitch rack and swung onto his saddle. He reined his gelding into the street and put him into a trot, heading for Pagosa Springs.

He intended to swing through Durango at the end of the week. If he didn't find Hawk there, he'd head south and east to Santa Fe.

An hour after leaving Del Norte, he reined the claybank to a sudden halt and stared skyward.

A large flock of buzzards swirled over a meandering dry wash a half mile south of the trail. Probably only an animal carcass, but whatever it was had attracted as many buzzards as Morgan had ever seen at one time. Gideon Hawk had taught him to listen to his instincts, and his instincts were telling him to check it out.

He turned the horse off the trail and gigged it into a trot, cutting through the sage and wild mahogany, kicking up fine red dust in his wake. He hadn't ridden fifty yards before the fetor of rotting flesh wafted over him. The smell got so strong that, sixty yards before the wash, he raised his neckerchief over his mouth and nose. His eyes watered as, halting the black, he stared over the crumbling clay bank.

Eight human bodies lay at the bottom, piled in a loose clump, as if they'd been rolled down the bank like household trash. A dozen buzzards milled amongst the carcasses, regarding Morgan with their bulging black eyes and hooked, yellow beaks, shrieking angrily.

Several hopped away and flapped their ratty wings, awkwardly joining the others swirling in the air above the wash. Several held their ground, screeching at Morgan as they ripped chunks of bloody flesh from necks or gaping, purple chest cavities.

Most of the clothes had been torn away by the buzzards and other scavengers, limbs lacerated beyond recognition, eyeless heads nearly eaten down to the bone.

Morgan could tell that the bodies were male. That's about all he could tell. A few were wearing cartridge belts without guns in the holsters or bullets in the cartridge loops, which meant that other men had probably looted the bodies before dumping them into the wash. Several were missing boots.

Morgan turned his horse around, galloped back to the trail, and lowering the neckerchief, put the clay-bank into a trot toward Pagosa Springs. A half hour later, he traced the trail around the base of a red-rock bench and rode into the town. He slowed his horse to a walk and studied both sides of the wide main street lined with brick and adobe business establishments, a few constructed of unpainted, whipsawed lumber.

Only a few people were about. Several windows, including those of the bank, were covered with pine planks. A low, brick jailhouse sat between a saloon and a harness shop, a big red dog asleep on the sun-lit stoop. When Morgan pulled up to the hitch rack and swung down from the saddle, the red dog rose heavily on its bowed, arthritic legs, and gave several raspy barks as Morgan mounted the stoop and opened the jailhouse door.

"Shut up, Red!" yelled a big man sitting behind a desk of pine planks laid across stacked apple crates.

The big man's chair was turned so that he half-faced another man standing in one of the three cells at the back of the room. The cell's door was open, and the man in the cell was combing his thick, black hair with one hand, patting it smooth with the other.

He glanced at Morgan as the big hombre sitting

behind the desk, a briar pipe in one brown fist, said, "That goddamn dog's gonna be the death of me yet. Him and his goddamn barkin' startin' up straight outta nowhere!"

He was built like a rain barrel, probably in his late forties or early fifties. He wore a red-striped shirt and shabby hide vest to which a town marshal's star was pinned. A high-crowned, round-brimmed hat squashed his mop of gray curls. His eyes were small and set too close to his big, broken nose. He didn't seem tall, sitting there rocking back in his swivel chair, pipe in his fist. But his arms straining his cotton shirt were as large as the wheel hubs of a heavy-duty freight wagon.

As Morgan stepped into the room and removed his hat, the big man's eyes found the U.S. marshal's badge on Morgan's fawn vest. "Well, whatd'ya know?"

"I'm Luke Morgan, deputy United States marshal," Morgan said crisply. "You the law here?"

The man lifted his red cheeks in a half wince as he studied Morgan's long, smooth, freckled face and serious eyes mantled by thin red brows. "I reckon I am . . . for the time bein'."

"What does that mean?"

"It means I'm the deputy town marshal from over at Del Norte. I'm a part-timer. The marshal *there* sent me over to keep a lid on things till the city council *here* can assign another man to the job."

"What's your name?"

"Colburn." The big man dropped his gaze again to

Morgan's badge, then to his dusty but otherwise neat whipcord trousers and high-topped black boots. As he stood, his eyes lingered on the two pearl-gripped Army Colts in the young lawman's tied-down holsters. "Say, if Ole Henry Peebles got hisself in trouble with the feds, I don't know nothin'—"

"Who's Peebles?"

"The town marshal. Least he was. He's dead, kilt by bank robbers near two weeks ago. Him and the entire posse wiped out."

"Who are the dead men in the arroyo east of town?"

The old man flushed, looked down at the pipe he held in his fist resting against the scarred desk planks. "Those'd be the men who wiped out the posse."

"Who took out the bank robbers?"

Colburn jerked his head toward the man in the cell. "He did."

Morgan looked at the short, wiry Mexican with bloodshot eyes and a vaguely hangdog look. The man stopped combing his hair and now stood in the open cell door, facing the two lawmen. Flushing, he smiled and lifted a shoulder, averted his gaze from Morgan's.

"He's in here cause he stomped with his tail up three nights in a row, blowin' all his reward money." The town marshal wheezed a laugh. "Damn near took out an entire saloon single-handed, and him and a whore crashed the mayor's wife's brand-new surrey." Colburn laughed again. "Paid out his entire poke in whiskey, whores, and fines!"

The Mexican shrugged again. "Easy come, easy go, eh, amigos?"

Morgan studied the Mexican closely. "To have brought down so many men yourself, you must be very good with a gun, Mister, uh . . ."

"Zamacona." The Mexican had turned away to finish combing his hair in the mirror. "I can protect myself, Señor."

"Taking down that many men single-handed is quite a bit better than merely 'protecting yourself.'"

Zamacona turned to Morgan sharply. "Are you calling me a liar, lawman?"

Morgan held the man's angry stare. As he studied him with cool objectivity—as Hawk had taught him, not letting emotion skew his focus—the corners of his mouth rose with bemusement.

Colburn shuttled his gaze between the two men, then turned to face the Mexican. "Pull your horns in, Toribio. And haul your hay. I'm tired of feedin' your bean-eatin' ass!"

The Mexican stared for another three long seconds at Morgan. Slowly, he turned away, cursed in Spanish, lifted his right foot onto the edge of the cell's single cot, and slipped his comb into the well of his high-heeled boot.

Colburn turned to Morgan, leaned forward in his chair. "Now, listen, Deputy, about them bodies. Ya see, the undertaker was taken down with the rest of the posse, and I saw no reason why in hell I should—"

Morgan held up a hand. "I don't care how you care for the dead in Pagosa Springs, Marshal. I'm here because I'm looking for a rogue lawman named Gideon Hawk." He reached into his dusty frock coat and produced a photograph, which he set on the desk before Colburn. "This is what Hawk looked like as of two years ago. Please study it closely."

"I've heard of Hawk," Colburn said, holding the photograph at arm's length from his face. He blinked as if to clear his eyes. "Good-lookin' man. Don't look like the killer everybody says he is."

"Like I said, that picture was taken two years ago, when his wife and son were still alive. He's changed a lot since then."

"I reckon anyone would."

"You haven't seen him, then?"

"Hell, I'd tell you if I had. Some people think he's some sorta savior. Me, I think he just makes us lawmen look like fools."

Morgan had been watching the Mexican out of the corner of his right eye. The man had donned his sombrero and stepped out of the cell. He'd grabbed a tooled leather gun belt off a chair. Wrapping the belt around his waist, he crossed the office to the front door.

As the man opened the door, Morgan said in a loud, clear voice, "There's a very generous reward for any information leading to the arrest of Gideon Hawk, Marshal. Please spread the word."

Morgan saw by the light on the floor that the door was standing half open. He could tell by the man-shaped shadow that the Mexican had frozen halfway through the opening and that his head was turned toward the desk.

Morgan reached into his wallet. To Colburn, he said, "Here's my card. If anyone comes to you with any information about Hawk's whereabouts, please notify my office."

"That's all we need around here," Colburn said as Morgan watched the shadow move outside, heard the Mexican's boots on the boardwalk, the door latch behind him. "More trouble. From a crazy lawman, no less." Outside, the dog chuffed with annoyance and scratched its nails on the boards.

When Morgan had returned the photograph to an inside coat pocket, he bade the marshal good day and stepped outside. The dog was sound asleep in the sunlight angling under the porch roof. It lay on its side, its fat, round belly rising and falling sharply as it breathed. Its hackles rose up and down, showing its yellow canines as it chased rabbits in its sleep.

A soft, clipped whistle sounded from a corner of the jailhouse. Morgan turned to see the Mexican standing beside the stoop, glancing up and down the street. Zamacona turned to Morgan, jerked his head, then wheeled and disappeared behind the jailhouse wall.

Morgan gave the man a few seconds, then stepped around the corner. He watched Zamacona walk down the side of the building, past a small stack of split cordwood and a trash pile at the rear, and disappear into the sod, brush-roofed privy standing at the far end of the lot, at the edge of a shallow gully.

Morgan walked up to the privy. Deer antlers hung on the door. An eye appeared in the crack between two weathered boards. "All right, it was not me who took down the badmen. I want you to know, however, that the only reason it was *not* me is because Hawk beat me to it."

"Which way was he heading?"

"What about the *dinero*?"

Morgan reached into a pocket, slipped a ten-dollar gold piece between the boards.

"I can tell you not only where Señor Hawk was heading when I last saw him, but because I am a caballero of the country, I can tell you where he is heading *now*. But it will cost you another one of these."

Morgan studied the single red eye staring at him through the boards. His instinct told him the man was telling the truth.

He dug another coin from his pocket and poked it through the boards.

6.

TREACHEROUS TRAVEL

FOLLOWING a curving stage road in western Colorado, under a leaden sky spitting sleet, Gideon Hawk turned up the wool collar of his buckskin coat and urged his grulla into a lope. Sleet-beaded sage and rabbit brush lined the trace. All around, mesas and copper-faced rimrocks rose behind a damp, gauzy veil.

Hawk had been on the killers' trail for three days and, judging by the tracks gouging the road's hard mud, he was getting close.

"You stop those horses right there, mister, or we'll trim your wick right here and now!"

Three men stepped out from behind the rock snag lining both sides of the trail.

"Oh, no!" Gideon Hawk gasped, pulling back on the grulla's reins. Sometimes feigning weakness was the best way to gain the upper hand in a dustup. "Oh, God. Please don't shoot!"

One of the three men stepping out from the rocks along the trail grinned as he leveled his double-barreled shotgun at Hawk's belly. "Well, that's entirely up to you, now, ain't it?"

"Take what you want. Just please don't shoot me."

The man with the shotgun—a short, wiry, gray-bearded gent with a shapeless brown hat—thoroughly enjoyed his authority. His lower jaw slid from side to side and his small, colorless eyes fairly glittered. "Crawl down from that hurricane deck, and be quick about it. My finger's gettin' itchy."

Hawk fumbled with his reins, as if not quite sure what to do with them. Finally, he dropped them, and swung down from the saddle. He pretended his left foot got hung up in the stirrup. Stumbling, he dropped to his knees and threw his hands in the air.

"Take what you want. I'm just headin' home with beef money to give to my boss. It's been a long trail up from Denver City, and I just want to get back to the bunkhouse with the boys!"

The three men surrounding Hawk, who'd changed from his frock coat and vest to cotton shirt, black jeans, and chaps, glanced at each other.

"Beef money?" said the youngest man, who was aiming a Spencer rifle at Hawk's right temple.

Hawk swallowed and winced. "Ah, gosh. No, I meant—"

"Shut up," ordered the gray-bearded gent. "Pruitt, check the packhorse. I got us a feelin' we mighta just struck the mother lode, and we won't be spendin' our winter holed up in Old Man Savant's drafty bunkhouse, after all."

"Ah, shit. Please. Not the beef money. You're gonna get me fired!"

"I said shut up!" raged the gray-bearded man, swinging his shotgun out like a club. He brought it forward, giving Hawk's head a glancing blow, knocking his hat off.

Hawk twisted around and fell on his right shoulder, feigning more pain than he felt. Inwardly, he cursed his own carelessness. For the past three days he'd been so intent on trailing the gang that had raided the prospectors' camp near his cabin that he hadn't kept his eyes peeled for other road agents, always a threat this far out in the tall and uncut.

The tallest of the three, and wearing a tattered doeskin coat and red knit fingerless gloves, Pruitt moved around Hawk and headed for the packhorse standing hang-headed behind the grulla. The gray-bearded gent glanced after him. His brows arched with eager expectance. The youngest man was also watching Pruitt, though he kept his Spencer aimed at Hawk.

Knowing he probably wouldn't get a better opportunity, Hawk sprang to his haunches. He filled his fists from the two holsters on his hips, knocked the Spencer aside with his Russian, and drilled the kid with his Colt.

A heart shot.

As the kid stumbled back with an exasperated

sigh, his eyes snapping with disbelief, Hawk extended the Russian and squeezed the trigger. The gray-bearded gent had jumped with a start. Now he swung his shotgun toward Hawk. He didn't get the gun leveled before a neat round hole appeared in the right center of his weathered forehead, snapping his head back on his shoulders.

As he stumbled back, he dropped the shotgun's barrels and tripped both triggers. The shotgun exploded, blowing a pumpkin-sized hole in the grassy center of the two-track wagon road, about equal distance between Hawk and the gray-bearded gent's own shuffling feet.

Hawk didn't watch him go down. He sprang to both feet and pivoted 160 degrees, both pistols extended straight out from his shoulders. Both horses had already bolted off the trail and were galloping, reins trailing, across the sage-stippled northern bench.

Wide-eyed with shock, Pruitt extended his silver-plated, short-barreled Schofield at Gideon, and popped off a shot. The bullet sizzled the air just to the left of Hawk's head. Hawk triggered both his pistols, the Colt and the Russian leaping in his hands at the same time.

Both Pruitt's earlobes disappeared in a spray of pink vapor.

Pruitt screamed.

He dropped his pistol, staggered back three steps, and bowed his head, clapping his hands over his ears. His mouth drew wide, lips stretching back from his

broken, yellow teeth. He glanced up at Hawk, saw
Gideon moving toward him with both pistols leveled.
He gave another cry, turned, and stumbled down the
road.

Hawk drilled him through the back of his right
thigh.

Pruitt stumbled forward. Whimpering, he dropped
to his knees. Clapping his bloody right hand to his
bloody right thigh, he dropped to his left hip and
shoulder, grunting and cursing, eyes bright with fear
and fury.

"Goddamn you son of a sow-bellied whore!"

Hawk stood over him, feet spread, elbows
snugged against his ribs, both pistols angled down
from his belly. His face was cold, implacable. A fine
sleet fell from a gunmetal sky, ticking off Hawk's hat
and shoulders.

"Did you meet a large gang a few hours ago?"
Hawk had lost the gang's trail after a cold rain the
previous night. He figured they were heading for the
only town out here, but he wasn't sure, and he didn't
want to waste time backtracking.

The man stared at him, befuddlement mixing with
the fury in his brown, red-rimmed eyes.

His hat had fallen, and the white sleet-pellets
flecked his thin, red-blond curls.

"Did you?" Hawk prodded, edging his voice with
menace.

Pruitt winced. "You a lawman?"

"That's right."

"If I tell you, will you let me go?"

"You bet."

Pruitt winced again, clapped his free hand to one ear, and gave his head a toss, as if to shake the pain from the other. "W-we met 'em, all right. Gave 'em a wide berth, too, we did. If you're after them all by your lonesome, lawman, you ain't long for this world. Can't say I care, neither." He squeezed his eyes and kicked his legs, ground his heels into the trail. "Son of a bitch! Why'd you have to shoot my *ears* off?"

"Who are they?"

Pruitt glanced up at Hawk skeptically. "You don't know?"

"If I knew, I wouldn't be asking you, would I?"

"Shit, it's Ed La Salle and Babe Mayberry's bunch."

Hawk vaguely recalled hearing the names several years ago. "Babe Mayberry's the woman?"

"If you can call her that. She's damn near as mannish as Ole Ed. Wouldn't wanna cross either one of 'em." Pruitt swallowed and raked a clipped breath. "Wouldn't wanna be you . . . or the sheriff o' Skinners' Bottoms."

"They gonna lay up there for a while, are they?"

"Prob'ly just long enough to kill the sheriff," Pruitt said with a wicked chuckle. "Wick Haskell hanged Ed's brother, Bob, for rapin' and killin' a couple o' Mex sheepherder's daughters. That poor son of a bitch is about to reap what he sowed."

"You don't say," Hawk said, genuinely intrigued.

"And you are, too!" Pruitt lifted his left foot and brought it down hard, heel first. "Oh, *God,* this hurts."

Hawk squinted down the barrel of his Russian .44.

"Hey, you said you was gonna let me go!" Pruitt screamed, shielding his face with his hands.

"How can I be sure you'll mend your ways? Give up the life of crime and walk the straight and narrow?"

Pruitt adjusted his hands so he could see between them. Staring up at Hawk, his eyes turned dark with resignation. "Ah, shit. You're that one they call the Rogue Lawman, ain't you?"

"You called it."

The Russian roared. Pruitt slumped back against the road with a sharp, anguished grunt. The bullet between his eyes trickled blood in which the fine, falling sleet melted.

Hawk holstered his pistols and turned to rake his gaze off the north side of the road. About a quarter mile across the high, rolling bench stippled with sleet-soggy sage and wild mahogany, his two horses stood about thirty yards apart, reins dangling.

He turned west. The little village of Skinners' Bottoms would lie just over that next rise, between the two tabletop mesas barely visible through the mist. On the breeze he could smell the faint smell of piñon pine from the town's wood fires.

Hawk dragged the dead outlaws off the road, leaving them for the hawks and coyotes, then found their horses tied in a cluster of rocks and brush south of the trail. Unsaddling and releasing the outlaws' mounts—some rancher would no doubt pick them up in a day or two—he headed out to retrieve the grulla and his packhorse.

Ten minutes later, he gigged the grulla toward Skinners' Bottoms.

A half hour earlier, the eighteen outlaws led by Ed La Salle and Ed's half sister, Babe Mayberry, galloped around a long bend in the stage road above Skinners' Bottoms.

They descended a low hill and crossed a deep, dry ravine on a wooden bridge, their horses thundering off the rough pine planks turned slippery by the sleet that came down at a forty-five-degree angle.

The sky hovered low, turning darker as the afternoon waned. The wind bit at the gang's coats, buffeted their collars and scarves about their necks, threatened to rip their hats from their heads.

A hundred yards from the bridge, Ed La Salle reined his black horse to a halt and raised his right hand for the others to do likewise. La Salle held his reins in his right fist and gave his cold, black-eyed gaze to the town nestled in the sage and broom grass before him, in the wide notch between two towering, flat-topped, sandstone mesas.

The town wasn't much. A dozen or so business establishments, some brick, some log, others with unpainted whipsawed pine planks, with maybe thirty or forty log cabins scattered about the low cedar- and boulder-stippled knolls on either side. Half of the hovels looked abandoned, with their boarded-up windows or missing doors or the weeds grown up around their stone foundations. An adobe mission church stood sentinel on a high shelf left of the town, flanked by the convex sandstone ridge.

Blinking against the sleet, La Salle gigged his horse forward, held the animal to a walk as he entered the shaggy outskirts of the town. The rest of the gang followed, Babe following to his right, her long, deer-hide coat cloaking her barrel-shaped body, her broad-brimmed man's hat covering her head. Babe sucked a long, thin cigar that the sleet had long since extinguished.

La Salle swung his gaze left to right and back again, scrutinizing the shabby buildings along the wide main street—shabby, that is, except for a two-story adobe hotel with a small, wrought-iron balcony off each upstairs room, wooden shutters thrown back from the windows. THE VENUS HOTEL AND SALOON was painted in large, red letters above its covered front porch. Beside the hotel sat a mercantile, then a harness shop.

On the stoop of the harness shop, two men stood talking, a dun horse tied to the hitch rack before them. One was dressed like a drover, in rough-hewn trail clothes. The other wore a leather apron and held a broom. Seeing the gang, the man with the broom stopped talking, frowned, glanced at the drover, and flicked a finger out from his broom handle.

They both looked at the gang. La Salle nodded cordially at the two men, his blue snake eyes crinkling at the corners.

He turned his head to the other side of the street, to the millinery shop with frilly white curtains in the windows lamplit against the waning light.

La Salle stopped his horse. Beyond the millinery, sitting alone on a wide lot spotted with silver sage, rabbit brush, and the skunk cabbage poking up like erect, green penises, was a low, square building made of hand-adzed pine logs. Over its short boardwalk was a shake-roofed awning. A sign above the awning read simply SHERIFF.

La Salle pulled his horse up to the building, Babe riding just off his right stirrup, the eighteen other gang members spreading out loosely behind them.

Babe looked at La Salle, then turned her head toward the building, the windows on either side of the timbered door showing umber lamplight. "Knock-knock-knock," Babe called in her raspy, mannish voice. "Anybody home?"

A silhouette appeared in the window. When it disappeared, the door latch clicked and the door swung open with a rusty squawk. A young man stepped out, hatless, wearing a gun belt and holding a six-shooter down low at his side. A five-pointed star was pinned to his shirt pocket.

He stepped to the edge of the boardwalk, ran his gaze across the twenty riders gathered before the office. He was olive-skinned, in his early twenties, with short, brown hair parted on the right, a curl licking down over his left eye. He squinted his brown eyes against the sleet.

Dully, he said, "Can I help you?"

"Yes, you certainly can, sonny," Babe said, wheezing a laugh. "Yes, indeed."

La Salle's low, even voice rose in sharp contrast to

his more loquacious sister's. "Send the sheriff out here."

"The sheriff ain't here."

"Where is he?" Babe asked.

"Outta town."

"Outta town where?" La Salle asked.

"That ain't any of your business. I'm Deputy Rose, acting sheriff till Sheriff Haskell gets back. How can I help you?"

"You can't help us, sonny," La Salle said as he reached under the flap of his buffalo coat. He unsheathed his long-barreled Navy Colt, extended it over his horse's head, and thumbed the hammer back.

Young Deputy Rose's lower jaw dropped as he watched the revolver's maw bear down on him. He'd only begun to raise his six-shooter when La Salle's pistol popped, drilling the deputy's third shirt button down from his throat.

With a choked grunt, the deputy dropped his revolver. The slug flung him straight back off his feet. He hit the boardwalk with the back of his head, gave a shake, and lay still.

The rest of the gang drew their own weapons as their horses jerked at La Salle's shot. They looked around cautiously. La Salle turned his horse and, holding his gun in his right hand, glanced across the street.

The two men who'd been talking before the harness shop stared back at the gang, eyes dark with fear. The man with the broom said something to the other man, then turned, scurried into the shop, and slammed the door shut. A shade that announced CLOSED snapped down over the door's window.

Casting tense glances at the gang spread out before the sheriff's office, the drover tugged his battered hat down over his eyes, leapt off the boardwalk, ripped the reins off the hitch rack, and swung onto the dun. In seconds he was galloping westward down the soggy street, crouched low in his saddle and casting fearful glances over his right shoulder.

"You sure put a burr in his bonnet, Ed!" said one of the gang members with a laugh, staring after the fleeing rider while holding a carbine across his saddle bows.

"Look there, Ed," Babe said.

La Salle followed his half sister's pointing finger. A silhouetted figure was scuttling along the front of the Venus. The man held a rifle in his hands. Something shiny glinted on his chest.

He stopped, pressed his back to the saloon. As La Salle gigged his horse toward him, the man froze, turned, and disappeared through the saloon's batwing doors.

"Time for a drink, Ed?" Babe asked, gigging her horse abreast of La Salle's.

"Yeah," La Salle grumbled, the wind blowing his beard as his horse angled toward the saloon. His bushy brows furrowed over his black, deep-sunk eyes. "Time fer a drink."

7.

UNEXPECTED GUESTS

DEPUTY Deuce Stokeley hurried into the Venus Saloon, breathing hard, his round, clean-shaven face flushed with fear.

He cast a sheepish glance at the five Lazy R riders who'd been playing billiards or sparking the Venus whores since Texas fever had put them out of work two weeks ago. It wasn't easy, but he slowed to a more dignified pace, raised his chin, and tried to put some swagger into his step as he moved to the back of the room, where Deputy Lars Cushman sat in an overstuffed chair before the popping fireplace. A long, black cigar protruded from Cushman's grinning lips, his battered bowler hat shoved back on his head.

Cushman's favorite whore, Tiffany May, draped her slender, white arms around Cushman's neck, and bounced up and down on his right leg, talking baby talk to the big, white-haired deputy. Cushman had been drinking and cavorting since the sheriff had been called out of town yesterday afternoon.

Stokeley dropped to a knee beside the chair. On account of the girl, he tried to keep his voice from quivering.

"Lars, I think we got trouble."

Cushman tore his drink-bleary eyes from Tiffany May, who leaned forward to offer a good view of her breasts bobbing around inside the thin, flesh-colored dress, and frowned with annoyance. "Huh?"

"There's a whole passel o' riders outside." Stokeley squeezed the carbine in his hands as though he were wringing water from a wet shirt. "I think . . . I think they shot Curtis."

When Cushman just stared at him, his mind slow to comprehend the information through all the beer and whiskey, Stokeley straightened and angrily jerked his head toward the front of the room. He turned and retraced his steps, trying not to run or let his shoulders sag.

"Hey, Deputy," said one of the half-drunk drovers playing billiards under a copper chandelier. "You find out who fired that shot?"

When Stokeley didn't respond, one of the other riders muttered something he couldn't hear. The others chuckled. Billiard balls clattered.

Stokeley cast his gaze over the batwings, squinting his eyes against the cold breeze blowing the snow under the porch roof. The gang had gathered before the saloon—fifteen or so men dressed in ratty fur coats and battered hats, sitting astride lathered, hang-headed mustangs. Most of the riders sported beards or mustaches. They all looked as woolly as trash-heap lobos, and they were all holding guns. The gang's leader was barking orders, sending the men off in different directions.

Stokeley had just realized one of the riders was a woman when Lars Cushman, a good four or five inches taller than Stokeley, stepped up beside him to cast his gaze over the doors.

Stokeley grabbed Cushman's right arm and pulled him back behind the front wall, nearly knocking over a bull-horn coat rack to which the drovers' dusters and slickers clung.

"They shot Curtis," Stokeley whispered. "And I gotta bad feelin' they're comin' fer us!"

Cushman's voice was thick, as though he hadn't used it in a while. "You think that might be La Salle?"

Since the circuit judge had ordered the execution of young Bob La Salle last spring, for raping and killing the Mexican girls, the sheriff and deputies of Skinners' Bottoms had been expecting trouble from Bob's brother, Ed, and his half sister, Babe Mayberry, both rumored to be in Mexico. When no trouble arose after a couple of months, however, they'd forgotten about it, or at least stopped letting it trouble their sleep. Ed and Babe were probably lying dead in some Sonoran arroyo, killed by *rurales* or Apaches, their bones picked clean by *zopilates*.

"It ain't Santy Clause," Stokeley said.

"Shit," Lars said, peering over the batwings. "There's upwards of twenty hombres out there."

"What're we gonna do?"

"My, my, my." One of the drovers was peering out the big window to the right of the batwings, holding his hands to the glass to block out the light. "There sure are a lot of *hard cases* out there!" He turned toward the deputies, a mocking sneer turning up a mouth corner. "They look like they come to collect on a bill."

Stokeley and Cushman looked at each other. Stokeley swung his glance around the room. Several other drovers and two whores were heading for the window. Cushman's girl, Tiffany, stood beside an adobe post from which spicy-smelling *ristras* hung, holding a blanket across her slender, bare shoulders. Her hair had half-fallen from its bun. Worry had worked its way through the opium she'd smoked, to turn her eyes wide and dark.

"Who is it, Lars?"

"It's nothin', honey. You go on upstairs." Straightening his shoulders and sticking his chest out with false confidence, Cushman turned to Stokeley. "Go sit down. Act casual but tough. I'm gonna stand by the bar."

Stokeley watched Cushman turn, stride over to the girl, and kiss her cheek. "Go on upstairs, sugar. Ole Lars has everything under control."

When one of the drovers snorted, Cushman shot a look at him, his cheeks coloring angrily, then turned and walked over to the bar. He slid his .44 from its holster, opened the loading gate, and filled the safety hole with a shell from his cartridge belt. He gave the gun a twirl, bouncing it awkwardly off the side of his holster, then slipped it back in the sheath.

Leaning an elbow on the bar top, he grabbed a clean glass off the pyramid beside the jar of pickled pig's feet, filled it from a half-empty rye bottle standing in a puddle of spilled whiskey, and threw it back.

Meanwhile, Stokeley had sat down at a table about fifteen feet from the bar. He'd been sitting there five minutes ago, drinking beer and laying out a game of solitaire, when the pistol shot had bludgeoned the snowy silence.

Outside, horses nickered and stomped, and hoof thuds rose. Apparently, the horses were being led away to a livery barn, which meant the La Salle Gang—if it was *indeed* the La Salle Gang—intended to dig in for a while. The notion made Stokeley's heart beat even faster. He tried to summon calming thoughts—images of high mountain lakes and newborn babes and the like—to slow it.

None would come.

He kept seeing Bob La Salle standing atop the gallows with the hangman's noose around his neck, glaring down at the sheriff and Stokeley and the other deputies, assuring them that his older brother and stepsister, "two of the rawest, hardest, cutthroat-*meanest* outlaws on the Southwestern frontier," would "hunt you down, gouge out your eyeballs, cut off your tongues and cocks, skin you alive, hang you, then carve up your families with skinning knives, and burn down your houses."

Then Bob had winked. The trapdoor had opened. The crack of his neck had resounded around First Street like a pistol shot.

Stokeley wished Sheriff Haskell were here. A seasoned lawman, Haskell might figure a way out of this situation. Besides, Haskell had been the one who'd hunted down young Bob La Salle, had him tried for killing those señoritas. But Haskell was out to the T-Bar-T, investigating Indian rustlers. He wasn't due back before noon tomorrow.

With Curtis Rose dead, Stokeley and Cushman were on their own.

"Here they come," warned one of the drovers.

The five cowboys had gathered in a clump before the front window, some with cue sticks in their hands. Quirleys or cigars sagged from their lips. Several wore their hats tipped back on their heads. Their hair was mussed, eyes rheumy and bloodshot from drinking, smoking, and doing the mattress dance with the whores upstairs. A couple looked amused. Most looked like they were half-thinking about skinning out the back door.

One—a blond little puncher named Fugate but nicknamed "Fungus"—was still upstairs, with the black-haired, brown-eyed French girl, Dominique. Stokeley hadn't heard the bed above the bar squawking for a while. Fungus and the whore must have fallen asleep.

Stokeley wished he was asleep . . . a long ways away from here.

He stared at the batwings. Boots thumped on the stoop. A bearded face and wide, thick shoulders appeared a foot above the doors. The eyes were shaded by a wide-brimmed leather hat.

Stokeley swallowed, clutched his empty beer mug, which he'd drained moments after hearing the shot that had taken down Rose, and tried to steady his nerves. His rifle leaned against the table, six inches from his right arm. He averted his gaze, tried to look casual but tough. Lars was doing likewise, leaning his left elbow on the zinc bar top, sipping his whiskey as though pondering his next fishing trip.

Stokeley thought he could hear the big deputy's heart thumping through his scruffy underwear shirt.

The batwings squawked. Stokeley looked up.

The big, bearded man swaggered into the saloon and stopped, casting his gaze slowly across the room as ten or so men and the woman—a stout little hen with mannish features and short red curls stuffed under a slouch hat—fanned out behind him.

The Lazy R men had turned to regard the bunch warily, several still holding their pool cues, blinking their eyes as if to clear them. Two whores had taken refuge on the horsehair sofa against the far wall, holding their heavy winter robes closed around their bare shoulders and legs. Another sat slumped at a table, too drunk to raise her head.

"Well, look what we have here," said the big man. "Two more tin stars." He laughed, but there was no mirth in it. He'd raised the bottom of his bear coat above the walnut grips of two well-oiled Colt Navys.

Cushman kept his elbow on the bar, hiking his right hip out so that his pistol was handy. "Can we help you men?" he asked.

"You know who I am?"

Cushman glanced at Stokeley, then returned his gaze to La Salle. "Should I?"

"You sure as hell should. My name is Ed La Salle. This here is my half sister, Babe Mayberry. We're kin to Bob La Salle, the young man you hung last spring. Remember him?"

Cushman didn't say anything.

The woman looked at Stokeley. Her eyes were as hard and cold as her brother's. They gave the deputy's racing heart a little hitch. "Where's Haskell?"

Stokeley cleared his throat. "He was called out of town, ma'am. Should be back tomorrow mornin'. If you wanna wait and take this up with him, the hotel's got plenty o' rooms. The apron's out gettin' firewood, but . . ."

La Salle's booming voice cut him off. "Shut up, you fuckin' windbag!"

Cushman stepped away from the bar, his face flushed with anger. "You can't talk to us like that!"

Before La Salle could respond, the back door whined open, sending a cool draft through the room. Two men moved through the shadows, past the open stone staircase, and stopped at the far end of the bar. It was the big, shaggy-headed bartender, Max Beardon, and a tall hard case in a tattered, gray slicker, holding a long-barreled pistol to Beardon's head. The bartender cradled a load of split firewood. His hair and beard were damp with melted snow. He looked around the room with barely contained fury.

"Found this one out back, Ed," said the man in the gray slicker. "Says he's the weekday bartender."

"Big son of a bitch, ain't he?" Babe Mayberry observed, raising her cigar to her chapped lips while keeping the other hand on the revolver holstered on her right hip. She ran her heavy-lidded eyes up and down Beardon's brawny, apron-clad frame, his pin-striped sleeves rolled up his tattooed forearms. "That's okay. I like 'em big . . . and stupid."

"He can be our wood-fetcher," La Salle said. "It's gonna be a long night. We're gonna need a lot of wood."

"What the hell you want?" Beardon barked.

"I'll tell you later, big man," Babe said, puffing her cigar.

The other hard cases chuckled, as did a few of the Lazy R riders gathered on the other side of the billiard table, huddled up as if for protection. The two whores on the fainting couch sat half-facing each other, blanket-draped knees raised to their chins.

"Babe," La Salle admonished, "this ain't neither the time nor the place. We're here for Little Bob. Don't forget that."

"Who the hell's Little Bo—?" Beardon stopped himself. His face slackening, he glanced at the deputies, then returned his gaze to La Salle. "Ah, shit."

"Ah, shit," the hard case standing between and behind Ed and Babe said with a chuckle. "Ah, shit is right."

"Enough!" La Salle said, turning his eyes to Cushman, who stood in the same position as when Beardon had entered. As the man in the gray slicker disappeared through the saloon's back door, La Salle said, "To answer your question, big man, we're here to kill every goddamn lawman in this town. But these two here is lucky." He walked toward Cushman. "You wanna know why you're lucky?"

Cushman glanced at Stokeley, who sat frozen in his chair, his hands in his lap.

"Why's that?" Cushman asked, his eyes showing cautious relief.

"'Cause I'm gonna kill you a lot quicker'n I kill Haskell."

La Salle moved so quickly that Stokeley didn't realize the man had even drawn his pistols before a shot resounded around the room like an earth tremor. Cushman hadn't even had time to slap his own revolver's grips before he was stumbling backward, groaning and holding both hands to his belly, flames licking off his shirt and filling the room with the smell of burning flesh and wool. He tripped over a chair and sat down on the floor, kicking, screaming, and batting the fire with his hands.

La Salle stood over him, extended the other pistol, and fired two more quick shots through Cushman's chest. The blond deputy threw up his arms as if in surrender, and slammed his head against the floor. Blood pumped from the chest wounds like twin geysers.

The flames had been doused by the viscera curling from the gaping hole in his belly. His bloody shirt continued to smoke and turn black.

Between the first and last shots, less than four seconds had elapsed. Stokeley found himself sitting in his chair, hands in his lap, staring down at the bloody, smoking Cushman with his jaw hanging to his chest. When he looked up, Babe was aiming her own Smith & Wesson at him, the hammer cocked. She smiled snidely around her cigar, jerked her head toward the Spencer carbine leaning against Stokeley's table.

"Ain't you even gonna try fer it? Hell, you might as well *try* fer it!"

Stokeley stared down the .44's yawning maw. From somewhere came the sound of dribbling water. Someone laughed.

"Hell, look at that!" the man squealed. "He's pissed himself!"

Sudden fury sparked like flint.

Stokeley bolted up from his chair, knocked it over backward. He reached for the Spencer, got both hands around it. He heard an enraged scream and realized it was his own.

Babe smiled at him, gave him an encouraging wink. As he raised the Spencer's stock to his shoulder, her pistol spit smoke and flames.

Stokeley didn't feel the bullet that killed him a half second before he hit the floor.

Nor did he hear Ed La Salle say, "Well, now that that's done, let's have us a drink and wait fer Haskell."

8.

"HASKELL . . . THAT YOU?"

AN hour later, Gideon Hawk trotted his horse to the outskirts of town over which the early night had fallen. The sleet had turned to damp snow. It lay over Hawk and his two horses like a blanket, fluttered against his eyes like down from a feather pillow.

Halting his horse near a signpost, he reached over to wipe the snow from the wooden face. Large blue letters formed the words SKINNERS' BOTTOMS, COLORADO TERRITORY, EST. 1866.

Hawk straightened, his damp saddle squeaking beneath him, and looked over the town. He couldn't see much behind the gray veil of falling snow besides a few yellow-lighted windows and the silhouettes of false facades. From somewhere came the tinny clatter of a piano, a lonesome sound amidst the sighing wind and whispering snow.

Cabins and shanties huddled in the low, rocky, brush-covered hills behind the business establishments. A few had wan light in their windows; most were dark. Somewhere in the hills to Hawk's right, a dog barked.

He leaned forward, resting his hands on the saddle horn, and thoughtfully chewed his snow-rimmed mustache. Best stay off the main street. A stranger in town would arouse La Salle's suspicions.

He reined his horses right, heeling the grulla into a trot, riding through the cabins and shanties huddled in the low, brushy knolls flanking the main drag. A barn loomed in the semidarkness, several blackbirds hunkered on the peak of its shake-shingled roof. Three corrals flanked the barn and a lean-to side shed. The barn's big front doors were open about a foot; in the gap, wan lamplight shone.

Hawk rode up and dismounted. He dallied the packhorse's lead line to his saddle horn, dropped the grulla's reins, and peered between the doors, smelling the hay and piss inside. A lantern hung on a square post about midway down the alley, spreading flickering light onto the straw-littered earthen floor.

On both sides of the alley, horses peered at Hawk over their stall partitions. He heard them breathing. Beyond the light at the other end, a shadow moved.

Hawk cleared his throat. "Hello?"

The only answer was a blackbird slapping a wing

against the roof, a cat's sharp meow somewhere to Hawk's left.

As he stared into the shadows, Hawk flicked the safety strap from his Russian's hammer. "I wanna stable my horses. You got room?"

After a few seconds, a man's shadow moved out from behind a stall at the back of the barn, where several buggies and wagons were parked, tongues hanging. After a few more seconds, the man began walking toward Hawk, his shadow growing in the shadows.

As the figure entered the lantern light, a young man took shape—hay-colored hair, freckle-faced, loose-jawed. Hawk figured he was fifteen or sixteen. He wore dung-smeared coveralls with one patched knee, and hobnailed boots. His hair was mussed; his lower lip was puffed up from a recent bruise.

"You work here?" Hawk asked, keeping his hand near his Russian's grips, darting his gaze cautiously around the barn.

The kid's voice was raspy and halting. "Y-you wanna stable your horse?"

Hawk stepped into the barn. He took one step to his left, so he wouldn't be backlighted. "Horses. I got two of 'em. Looks like you're filled up."

"I got room in the lean-to," the kid said, moving slowly toward Hawk, his arms hanging straight down at his sides. "If they can share a stable . . ."

"That'd do." Hawk took another look around the barn, then turned, pushed the right door wide, went out, and grabbed the grulla's reins. He led the horses inside, and handed the grulla's reins to the boy.

"Give 'em a goodly portion of oats, will you, boy?" Hawk shucked his Henry from the saddle boot and strolled down the barn alley behind the boy, inspecting the horses hanging their heads over the stable doors. "And curry 'em . . . if you got time."

"I reckon I got all night," the boy said, reaching under the grulla's belly for the latigo buckle.

"A lot of horses here," Hawk observed.

The boy didn't say anything.

"A big group pull into town recently?"

The boy slipped the saddle from the grulla's back. He stopped and turned to Hawk. The light was too uncertain for Hawk to see his face. The boy turned slowly, took several steps, and set the saddle on a rack.

"These horses here?" the boy said. "These are just the lendin' stock."

"That's a lot of lendin' stock for a town this size." Hawk reached over a door and ran his hand down a mustang's left shoulder, fingered the tack resting over the stall's thin pine wall. "This horse is warm and his tack is wet."

Hawk strolled back to the boy, who stood before the grulla, the conflicting drafts shunting the lantern light across his worried face.

"They do that to you?" Hawk said, nodding at the kid's cut and swollen lip.

"Please, mister . . . they said if I said anything,

they'd burn the barn down. This here livery's all me and my folks have."

Hawk stopped before the boy, gazed down at him. "I don't aim to let that happen, son. They came here to kill the sheriff. I'm here to stop that from happening, too."

The boy frowned. "You a lawman?"

"You might say that. They mention where they were headed when they left here?"

The boy shook his head. "Three men brought the horses. Just after I heard a pistol shot up by First Street. They were walkin' outta the barn when I heard more shootin'. One of 'em laughed and said somethin' about a fandango at the hotel. They couldn't have got the sheriff, though. He's outta town till tomorrow. I take care of his horse."

"Hotel's on the main drag?"

The boy nodded. "Biggest building."

"What about the sheriff's office?"

"South edge of town, west side of the street."

"Obliged, boy. I'll be back tomorrow morning for my horses." Hawk flipped a coin in the air. The kid caught it with both hands.

As Hawk walked down the barn alley and opened the back door, the kid's voice rose behind him. "Hey, you ain't gonna try to take down the whole gang by yourself, are you?"

Hawk paused, then stepped outside, shut the door behind him, raised his fur collar, and looked around. When he'd gotten his bearings, he traced a circuitous route north, passing several abandoned cabins and empty wagons grown up with brush and weeds. The snow had grown heavier, making the footing tricky where it had begun to lay.

He moved along the backside of First Street until the buildings began to thin at the town's west end. He swung up to the main drag and hunkered down behind a barrel along a building's side wall. On the other side of the street stood a two-story adobe that had obviously been built in more prosperous times, with recessed windows and wrought-iron balconies off the second-story rooms, red tiles adorning the gracefully pitched roof.

Big letters stretched above the front stoop announced THE VENUS HOTEL AND SALOON. The large, first-story, gilt-edged windows were brightly lit, man-shaped shadows moving behind them, several with their hatted heads tipped back, mouths drawn wide. Laughter and the clatter of billiard balls spilled through the doors.

The piano was being pounded in earnest now, by someone who made up in vigor what they lacked in talent. A screechy voice of indeterminate sex sang loudly, the words garbled by the other voices and by the wind funneling down the street, squawking shingle chains and banging shutters.

Hawk turned right and jogged, crouching along the south side of the street. He stayed close to the building shadows, following the sporadic stretches of boardwalk for fifty yards before the sheriff's shingle showed through the snowy darkness. A light shone in

the log building's side window. Smoke ruffled from
the tin chimney pipe.

Hawk hunkered down on his haunches before a
woman's hat shop. Facing the jailhouse, he took a
long, slow look around. Nothing out here but snow
knifing the thickening night and bits of soggy trash
swept down the main drag to his left.

Leaping off the boardwalk, he jogged across the
shaggy trail that served as a side street, and pressed
his back to the side wall of the sheriff's office, left of
the square, sashed window. Keeping his right shoulder pressed against the wall, he sidled a glance
through the foggy pane, beyond which two men sat
across from each other across a broad pine desk.
Both men wore shabby fur coats, and both were
bearded. One wore a mud-streaked top hat with a
damp feather sticking up from the band.

The men were playing two-handed poker, each
with a pistol near his elbow.

Beyond them, near the door, another man lay on
the floor, in a puddle of thick blood. Blood stained
his chest, nearly hiding the five-pointed star pinned
to his shirt pocket. His head was tipped toward the
window, his open eyes appearing to hold Hawk's
gaze, as though silently asking for help.

The man wearing the top hat stood suddenly and
slapped his cards on the table. Hawk pulled his gaze
back, flattened his back against the wall.

". . . this time," the raised voice sounded through
the window. "But next time, it's your turn no matter
how many hands you win!"

The other man laughed.

Boots thumped on the puncheons, vibrating the logs against Hawk's spine. Hawk turned left and, following the footsteps, walked to the building's rear corner and stopped. At the back of the building, a door latch clicked, hinges squeaked.

"Shit!" the cardplayer grumbled.

There was a scuffing sound, a grunt, the slap of a hand against wood. Apparently, the man had slipped as he'd stepped out of the jailhouse. He cursed again, sighed heavily. No sound for a moment, then crunching footsteps and breathing.

Hawk peered around the corner. The man in the top hat and deerskin coat, a red knit sweater wrapped around his neck, stomped toward a woodpile to the right of an unpainted privy constructed of split, upright pine logs.

Holding his rifle in both hands across his chest, Hawk put his right foot forward. It snapped a snow-covered sage branch—a muffled crunch. To his right, the cardplayer froze and began turning. Hawk threw himself back behind the jailhouse wall.

Silence.

Hawk heard the man breathing.

"Haskell . . . that you?" The cardplayer's voice was tentative, thick with drink, half-mocking.

Hawk pressed his back against the wall, squeezed his rifle in his hands. After about five seconds, the man turned and began walking toward the woodpile. He lifted the damp, burlap tarp from the wood, and began filling his arms with split stove wood.

When he had seven logs stacked across his chest, he turned carefully, blinking against the falling snow, and made his way back toward the door he'd left open and which the wind slapped against the outside wall.

"So Flamenco is better at two-handed poker," he grumbled as he set his feet carefully down in the thickening snow. "Does that mean he's gonna sit inside all night, warm and cozy, while I freeze my oysters gatherin' firewood to keep his Nueces River ass from catchin' cold?" He snorted with disgust. "I say, who's the better *pistol shot*? Ha!"

He stopped before the door frame, gently shifted the weight of his load to his left arm. Reaching for the door's inside knob with his right hand, he stepped into the cabin, drawing the door closed behind him.

He hadn't gotten it halfway closed before a brass-plated rifle butt, appearing out of nowhere, shot toward his face. His jaw dropped as the butt smashed his nose flat against his right cheekbone, both lips popping like blood-filled water balloons.

As he stumbled back into the yard, the wood fell from his arms, clattered onto the jailhouse floor, several logs rolling onto the ground. As he reached for the pistol on his right hip, the rifle butt shot forward again, connecting this time with his forehead.

His lights dimmed. His feet slipped out from under him. His back hit the ground.

Hawk stepped out of the jailhouse, stood over the big man groaning in the jailhouse yard. He lowered his rifle, crouched over the man, who moved his bloody face from side to side, the nose bent back across the cheekbone. Hawk glanced at the open door, where a dim light shone in the building's bowels.

Hearing no movement from within, Hawk turned to the whimpering man on the ground before him.

"What's your name?"

The man choked, kicked a foot feebly. "Merle Pugh."

"Thought I'd recognized you."

A few years ago, Pugh had killed three Indian men in eastern Dakota Territory, stolen their horses, kidnapped the girl who'd been traveling with the men. He'd gone on a killing spree south to the Arkansas River, where Hawk had lost his trail, finding the Indian girl, battered and bloody beyond recognition, at the bottom of a whiskey peddler's privy.

"Who the fuck are you?" Pugh asked, spitting blood and slapping his right arm against the ground as pain racked him.

Hawk stood, stared down at Pugh, then rammed his rifle butt once more across Pugh's forehead. When he lifted the butt from the caved-in skull, Pugh's eyes stared up at him glassily.

"The man that just blew out your worthless lamp," Hawk muttered as he turned and stepped into the jailhouse, reaching behind his neck and grabbing his horn-handled stiletto.

9.

A WOMAN OF DIVERSE

DESIRES

IN the Venus, Babe Mayberry was pounding the beat-up piano, draped with a tattered Confederate flag, and singing loudly and hoarsely:

> *Several years ago I met a sweet boy, Pete.*
> *Oh, he was a shy one, Pete.*
> *But I gave him time, and taught him well,*
> *And he came to fuck me sweet!*

She lifted her head with its dimpled chin and broad, pimpled nose, drawing out the "sweet" until her voice cracked. She ended the song with a few, quick, punctuating notes, cackling and dropping her gaze to the snaggle-toothed rustler, Boone Logan, and the flat-faced half-breed everyone called Co-manche.

The men had been dancing before the fireplace in the saloon's rear wall, to Babe's tunes. They hadn't always been dancing in step with the tunes, nor with each other, but they'd been dancing a bizarre hybrid of barn dance, polka, and wrestling match with a goodly bit of Indian powwow thrown in. Whiskey sloshed in the bottles that they gripped by the necks, periodically tossing their heads back and throwing down a drink, squinting their eyes at the alcohol's burn and loosing a jubilant whoop at the rafters.

Babe and the men had all been on the trail for nearly a month, since getting word, deep in Mexico, that Little Bob had been hanged in Skinners' Bottoms. In that time, they hadn't had a roof over their heads, much less a bed beneath their backs. Needless to add, they hadn't had their ashes hauled since Mexico, neither—a little matter several of them were upstairs rectifying at this very moment.

The saloon's adobe walls and ceilings were thick, but every once in a while the squawk of a bedspring could be heard, or the quick, horrified protest of a Venus working girl, doubtless ill prepared for the intensity of the La Salle riders' carnal hunger.

Tired from the long ride herself, and from the half quart of whiskey she'd downed since arriving in town two hours ago, Babe sat up straight on the piano bench and stretched her arms out before her, cracking each knuckle in turn. Though the music had stopped, the two dancers continued dancing, half out on their feet, muttering their own lyrics in their heads.

The fire snapped and popped. The wind moaned in the chimney, sucked at the flames.

Babe plucked her cigar from the ashtray atop the piano, stood, and looked around the room. It would be a long night, and she needed another diversion.

Several of the boys were stretched out on the floor before the fire, catching some shut-eye, hats over their eyes. Several others just sat drinking and staring into the flames.

At a table near the bar, Ed and four others were playing poker with the gold and silver they'd robbed from an Army payroll wagon near Contention City. To Babe's right, the five Lazy R drovers sat hog-tied against the side wall, gagged not so much so they couldn't yell out, warning Haskell, but so they couldn't complain about having the circulation to their hands and feet cut off.

The man who'd been ordered to keep an eye on the five prisoners, a tall, patch-bearded kid named Alvis Turner, sat in a deep-cushioned chair nearby. A girl straddled Alvis's lap, facing him, her exposed chest even with Alvis's long, pale face.

Alvis had the girl's dress pulled down so low that both nipples showed just above the red satin fabric. The skirt was drawn up above her thighs, bunched around her waist. As Alvis ran one hand up and down the girl's creamy right thigh, he pinched her nipple between the index and thumb of his left hand.

"That's some stuff," Alvis was muttering, running

his eyes over the girl's breasts. "Oh, yeah. That's some stuff."

The girl said nothing, her face expressionless, almost bored. She was looking into space somewhere toward the bar, before which the big, burly barman had been ordered to sit on a high stool, near the card-players. He was allowed to move only to bring more bottles to the table, or to empty ashtrays or light cigars.

Ed had ordered several men to ransack the back bar, cleaning out any weapons they found, which included a bung starter, a double-barreled shotgun, and a rusty bowie knife.

A good-looking gent, that barman, Babe thought, giving the big man the twice-over with her eyes. But Ed wouldn't let him out of his sight. Babe turned to Comanche, dancing broad circles behind the chairs forming a semicircle before the fire. Comanche was the one Babe most often called when she needed a stiff shaft between her wheels—but when he'd been drinking as much as he had tonight, he wasn't always a gentleman.

Not that Babe was afraid of him. He was just too valuable a long rider for Babe to have to pop off a pistol in his ear.

"When Jobel comes down," Alvis Turner was telling the disinterested whore in his lap, "you and me gonna go upstairs and get down to *business*!"

Babe took a long puff from her cigar, blew the smoke straight out before her. Glancing around, she noticed that the girl sitting at the gambling table, on

Bryce Pope's lap—a pudgy, round-faced little waif named Camille—was staring at her. Babe had caught the girl looking at her before, meeting Babe's gaze briefly, then turning her head and lowering her gaze to the poker table.

Bryce had taken the girl upstairs, then brought her down and made her sit with him. Bryce was like that. He'd get fixated on one whore, and want her available only to him all night long.

Babe felt an irritated burn in her gut.

She stuck the cigar in her mouth, hitched her duck pants on her broad hips, adjusted her pistol belt, and sauntered up to the gambling table.

"I wanna bath," she barked at the girl. "And I want you to heat the water and fill the tub."

"Hey, wait now, Babe," Bryce said, his big, dark face coloring up, his single eyebrow forming an inverted V above his nose. "This one's—"

"Shut up, Pope!" Babe barked, grabbing the girl's bare arm and jerking her off Bryce's lap. "I wanna bath and I want her to heat the water. You wanna blow some smoke over it?"

As the girl gave a distressed little grunt and twirled away from the table, turning to regard Babe and Pope fearfully, Pope narrowed his eyes at Babe, set his jaws with anger. He shuttled his glance across the table to Ed La Salle, who grinned over the pasteboards spread out in his hands.

There was a flinty little glint far back in La Salle's gaze. Everyone who knew La Salle knew that glint, and had either come to respect it or gone to meet their Maker.

"When it comes to Babe," Ed growled through his grin, "you gotta take the tail with the hide."

Pope looked back at Babe, who stood to his right, her feet spread, her coat thrust back behind her pistol butt. He looked at his right hand again, lowered it, and sighed. He drew closer to the table.

"Where was we, goddamnit? Now I'm all distracted."

Smiling victoriously, Babe removed her cigar and turned to the girl. "You heard me, peach. Run and fetch me some water, and haul it upstairs. Best room you got. If they's humpin' in there, kick 'em out. Tell 'em Babe's orders!"

Babe laughed as the girl ran into the kitchen behind the bar, and sauntered up to the zinc-topped mahogany. "Hey, big man," Babe told the glowering barman, "I wanna bottle o' port."

"You won't find port or anything like it this side of Denver City," the barman said, showing his teeth as he spoke very slowly and precisely.

"No?" Babe said, ignoring his insolence. "Whatcha got that's close?"

"Closest thing I got to port is sangria."

Babe stuck her cigar in her teeth, threw her head back, cackled, and clapped her hands. "Hell, I *love* sangria!"

When she had her straw-jacketed, long-necked bottle in hand, she followed the whore, Camille, up the staircase at the back of the room.

"Don't let her outta your sight, Babe," La Salle yelled after her. "I gotta man at the back door, but I don't want *no one* slippin' out and warnin' Haskell."

"You watch your own whores, brother," Babe retorted. "I'll watch mine!"

She cackled and continued following the girl up the stairs and into the largest room in the hotel, outfitted with its own fireplace and real feather bed, at the far south end of the hall. She had to kick another whore and a bleary-eyed old renegade named Horace Bender out of the room, gamy with the smell of sex and Bender's sweat, but it was worth it.

The room was warm from the snapping fire, and umber-lighted by the flames and the red-globed lamps flickering atop the heavy wooden furniture, including a broad, marble-topped dresser. Three steps rose to the shuttered balcony facing the side street, making the bed seem as though it lay at the bottom of a broad bowl.

A huge copper tub with a built-in seat glistened before the fire. While Camille made several trips from the downstairs boiler, filling the tub, Babe stripped down to her long underwear, and sat in a deep, red chair near the fire, sipping sangria from the bottle and languidly smoking her cigar. She watched the half-naked girl fill the tub, admiring the way the girl's thighs rippled when she hefted the bucket, the way her dress bowed out from her chest, revealing the full, heavy breasts.

When the tub was full and steaming, Babe ordered the girl to undress before her. As Camille did so,

Babe watching from the chair, thick ankles crossed, wriggling her stubby toes, Babe said wistfully, "I seen you lookin' at me down there."

"You did?" the girl said, brown eyes flashing false surprise.

"You like other girls, do you?"

"I reckon I can stand a stiff rod now and then," the girl said, stepping out of her dress, stooping to pick it up, folding it lengthwise, and laying it over a chair. "But all the bullshit you have to put up with—the bad smells and the whisker burns, not to mention the bragging, and how you have to keep tellin' 'em how great they are or they'll start shootin' over the balcony. . . . Makes me prefer a woman's gentle touch now and then."

Babe was wheezing with laughter, shaking her head. "Ain't that the truth?"

Demurely, the girl glanced at Babe. "I had a feeling, under that gruff exterior, you were . . . I don't know . . . sensitive. . . ." Standing naked before Babe, the round-faced girl shrugged and stared down at her toes.

Babe let her laughter die. She took a deep drag off the cigar, stubbed it out in the glass ashtray atop the low table beside the chair. "Why don't you climb on into the tub and let me wash all that fine skin of yourn?"

When the girl had climbed down into the steaming water, Babe took her time, bathing the girl with a soapy sponge, exploring every nook, cranny, and crevice. The girl cooed and shivered, threw her head back with pleasure.

When Babe had finished bathing the girl, she stripped and climbed into the tub's opposite end, both of them laughing as the water exploded over the rim, gurgling across the floor, soaking the Chinese rug. They shared a glass of wine and another cigar, and then the girl sponged Babe the way Babe had sponged her.

They got so worked up that, when they'd been in the tub for the better part of an hour, they hurried out, gave each other a cursory rubdown with a towel, and jumped into the bed. Babe was so hot, she didn't even care that the sheets still smelled like Horace Bender.

"Turn onto your belly," the girl said in a husky, sensuous voice.

"What's that?" Babe said, gooseflesh rippling all over her pale, stout body, lifting her legs and curling her toes with desire.

"Turn over. You're in for a real treat, Babe."

"Well, all right. If you say so."

Babe turned onto her belly, bunched a pillow beneath her big, flaccid breasts, so that they ballooned up around her neck. She felt the girl get off the bed, heard a bare foot slap the stone floor.

"Where you goin' honey?"

"Just to get some oil."

"Oil!" Babe laughed. "Oooh—I like that."

"You'll love this," the girl said, climbing back onto the bed and straddling Babe's broad, dimpled butt. Liquid sloshed in a bottle. "It'll be just a little cool at first . . ."

"That's all right," Babe said. "You'll warm it up right quick, won't ye, hon—?" She'd slid her gaze to the right. In a mirror hanging above the dresser, she saw the girl holding something with both hands, high above Babe's head. It was the sangria bottle.

"Hey, what—?"

The girl grunted. In the mirror, the bottle dropped in a shadowy blur. Babe heard the glass break at the same time she felt the bottle's heel slam against her head, felt the cool, thick wash of sangria in her hair, running down her neck and across her shoulders.

Her eyeballs burst with a dazzle of light. Pain shot through her. She gritted her teeth, felt herself passing out, and fought against it.

She rose onto her right shoulder, shrieking, "You . . . little . . . *bitch!*"

She'd moved just in time to avoid the bullet that plunked into the bed where her spine had been a half second before. Her ears were still ringing from the bottle, so she'd only half-heard the shot. As it echoed around the room, Babe looked toward the end of the bed.

Camille stood, her dress thrown over her naked right shoulder, extending her arms straight out from her face, aiming Babe's pistol in both shaking hands. Her face was bunched with fury and desperation, tears streaking her cheeks.

She sobbed, bit her lip, and tried to steady the pistol.

Babe flung herself back off the bed as the revolver exploded, flames and smoke stabbing from the barrel. The slug blew up more feathers from the mattress before grinding into the floor beneath the bed.

The girl screamed and slid the revolver toward Babe.

As the big woman lifted her pudgy knees to her chest and buried her head in her arms, the pistol popped again, the slug drilling into the wall over Babe's head, spraying her with bits of adobe.

The girl screamed and, wheeling toward the door, threw the gun at Babe. It glanced off the woman's left elbow and scuttled across the floor.

Babe raised her head. The girl was fumbling with the door. She pulled it open, then holding her dress in her right hand, bolted through the doorway, her left foot slipping out from beneath her, nearly causing her to fall as she swung right and disappeared down the hall.

"You fuckin' little trollop!" Babe squealed, clambering onto her hands and knees, then heaving herself to her bare feet. She stooped for the gun and, too furious to bother with clothes, marched across the room and through the open door.

"What the hell's all the shootin' about?" asked one of the gang members, standing naked in an open door on the other side of the hall, a pistol in his hand.

Ignoring him, Babe strode down the hall like a confident soldier striding off to war. Ahead of her, Camille crouched through a small door in the wall on the left side of the hall. The door had been disguised with wainscoting and wallpaper. It boasted a little decorative fob for a knob.

Babe jerked it wide open and, lips pooched out with rage, stared into the musty, stygian darkness, hearing the soft thuds of bare, running feet below.

There was the click of a latch. Dim gray light shone in the stairwell's depth.

"Oh, no, you don't!" Babe bellowed. "You're *not* getting away from *me,* you little trollop!"

Babe was at the bottom of the curving, low-ceilinged well in no time. She pushed out the door, found herself on the snowy side street. Squinting against the snow and the wind, ignoring the cold sangria dribbling down her back, she saw the girl's small, shadowy figure angling away from her.

The girl was running kitty-corner across the main street, in the general direction of the sheriff's office. The light in the jailhouse silhouetted her.

"Get back here and take your medicine, girl!" Babe raged, putting her head down and breaking into a run, her Colt in her right hand.

When she was about twenty yards from the fleeing whore, the light in the sheriff's office suddenly went out. Babe was puzzled by that, but the girl was foremost on her mind. Even without the backlight, she could make out Camille's retreating figure—a dark, bobbing, swaying blur straight ahead of her.

Babe stopped and raised the pistol.

Planting her bare feet, she extended her right arm, sighted down the barrel, and fired.

Without so much as a cry, the girl dropped, sliding

several yards along in the mud and snow before coming to rest about thirty yards from the jailhouse's front stoop.

Hearing voices and boots crunching snow behind her, Babe walked up to the girl and stared down. The bullet had nearly blown the top of the little trollop's head clean off.

Babe snorted, swung her right foot back, then slammed it forward against the girl's bare back. "Take that, you miserable witch."

Tears came to her eyes and she felt her chest heave with a sob. It surprised her. She choked back another sob, wiped tears from her cheek with the back of her gun hand.

Turning, she limped back the way she'd come.

"What the hell happened, sister?" asked Ed La Salle, cautiously moving into the street with several other men from the saloon. He had his pistol out and was crabbing sideways and jerking his head around, wary of an ambush.

"Shot me a connivin' whore's all," Babe said, brushing past him, not bothering to cover her flopping, swaying breasts even when she passed the others.

She turned her head to call over her shoulder, "Better check out the jailhouse, Ed. Somethin' fishy's goin' on over there."

10.

SHERIFF'S OFFICE

HOLDING the horn-handled stiletto in his right hand, the rifle in his left, Hawk made his way toward the light at the end of the cell block's hall, moving lightly on the balls of his boots. To his right, the three cells' iron doors and padlocks glistened dully in the wan light streaming in from the main office.

Ahead, the wooden door to the main office stood halfway open. Hawk stopped before it and, holding his breath, pulled it slowly toward him, surprised and relieved to find that the hinges didn't squeak.

When the door was three quarters open, Hawk stood silently, raking his gaze around the lamplit room. The dead man's partner sat where Hawk had last seen him, behind the desk, his back to the cell block door. He was leaning back in his chair, his left ankle crossed on his right knee, holding a tin cup up to the lantern light, as if admiring the wash of the light on the whiskey. His pistol lay on the desk, its walnut grips angled toward his bulging belly. His pasteboards lay facedown before him.

Against the log wall to his right, the wood stove ticked and cracked quietly as it burned, the small wood box beside it holding only a few short kindling sticks and a single split cottonwood log.

Hawk carefully leaned his rifle against the wall to his left, and moved forward, setting each boot down quietly. He was three feet from the desk when the man, having sipped his whiskey, set his cup down.

He ran the back of his left hand across his mouth and turned toward the back of the room. "God-damnit, Pugh, what the hell is takin'—?"

He was only half-turned, an impatient expression on his face, when he saw Hawk. He froze, eyes snapping wide.

He jerked back toward the desk, thrust his right hand at the Remington. As he wrapped his fingers around the butt, Hawk stepped smoothly forward, grabbed the man's hair through his hat, jerked his head back, and cleanly swept the stiletto blade across the man's beard-bristled throat.

The man's Remington clattered to the floor as he raised his hands to his neck and kicked the chair back against the wall, jumping around as though he'd been struck by lightning.

He gagged and choked, eyes at once enraged and horrified. Blood gushed from his jugular, spurting across the room and splashing the wood stove, sizzling and smoking the instant it hit the hot iron.

Stepping back from the blood flow, Hawk stooped to retrieve the man's pistol, but stopped when running footsteps sounded outside, making splashing, crunching sounds in the snow and mud.

Hawk straightened, listening.

"Get back here and take your medicine, girl!" someone shouted in a raspy, enraged voice.

Hawk leaned quickly toward the desk, and blew out the lamp. He dashed to the back of the room for his rifle, then leapt the spilled blood to the room's front window.

Shoving the shade back with his Henry's barrel he peered into the dim, snowy street. He saw the silhouette of the girl running toward him a second before a gun flashed behind her.

The pop echoed flatly, like a snapped twig.

The girl dropped, skidded several feet along the street. Against the lights of the hotel behind her, Hawk saw the splash of the mud and snow. The girl's limbs flopped to the ground and lay still.

About twenty or so yards from the hotel, the bulky figure that had fired the pistol walked toward the girl sprawled in the street. In the dim light, she appeared to be a fat, naked woman with short, curly hair. After a time, she turned, passed several figures moving in the direction of the sheriff's office. There was a brief exchange of conversation, too distant for Hawk to make out the words.

As the naked woman disappeared into the shadows of the hotel, several men spilled out the hotel's front doors and joined those already gathered in the street. They were talking and looking in Hawk's direction. One gestured at the sheriff's office, canted his head sharply right.

As he and three others, wearing fur coats or dusters and all wielding either rifles or pistols, moved toward the office, three more broke away from them, angling toward the building's rear.

"Pugh, Flamenco—you in there?" the leader called toward the office.

He was a tall, bearded man with a high-crowned hat and a bear coat. In his right hand, he aimed a long-barreled Navy Colt at the building. He walked slightly bowlegged toward the office, high-topped jack-boots splashing mud and slush, and reached under the coat's left flap and filled his other hand with another long-barreled Colt.

He and the other three were close enough now that Hawk could hear their boots squeak in the mud, hear the ratcheting of pistols being cocked. A metallic scrape sounded as a shell was rammed into a rifle breech.

Hawk glanced thoughtfully down at his rifle's forestock. Hearing muffled voices at the back of the office, he stepped over to the front door and slowly squeezed the knob until the latch clicked open. He drew the door wide, stepped onto the boardwalk.

Before him, the men heading toward the sheriff's office stopped in the street, about fifteen feet from the door. When they saw Hawk's silhouette, their bodies tensed.

Hawk aimed his Henry straight out from his hip and pulled the trigger, the rifle jumping, the barrel stabbing flames. The leader gave a clipped yell and twisted back, falling.

Hawk fired four more shots into the dispersing group, quickly levering the Henry as their surprised yells and curses rose amidst the booms. Several guns blossomed before him as the men returned fire, dodging his shots or dropping to their knees, wounded.

Their slugs buzzed around his head, thumping into the cabin and plunking through the window, adding the screech of breaking glass to the sudden cacophony.

As a shot sprayed wood slivers from an awning support just ahead of him and left, Hawk wheeled and ran around the other side of the cabin, hurdling snowcapped rabbit brush and sage. Near the end of the building, he stopped and pressed his back to the wall.

Inside, boots thumped as someone ran toward the main office. Outside, only a few feet away, running boots crunched snow and snapped sage branches. Someone spit loudly as they moved toward Hawk.

Hawk waited, squeezing the Henry in his gloved hands, pressing his spine and the back of his head to the lumpy logs. A shadow dashed toward him along the ground.

As a figure rounded the cabin's rear corner, Hawk

dropped to his knees and leaned forward. The man's shins slammed into Hawk's side. As the man grunted and fell forward, Hawk heaved himself up from his feet, lifting the man off his own feet, and flipping him end over end in the air.

The man lost his rifle and hit the ground with a groan.

Hawk stepped toward him. The man lifted his head, blinking his eyes and flailing blindly for his rifle. Hawk swung his right leg back and forward, his boot toe connecting savagely with the man's jaw, which broke with an audible *crack!*

The man's head smacked the ground with a thud, and his body lay still.

A gun shot blossomed in the corner of Hawk's left eye. The crack sounded a quarter second before Hawk felt the burning sting in his left arm. Hawk swung his rifle toward the front of the jailhouse and fired, hearing his slug thump into the building's front corner. Shadows jostled and men cursed.

With the same motion, Hawk swung left and around the corner of the building. Inside, boots pounded the floor, and the rear door swung wide.

Hawk stopped, extended the Henry, and fired two rounds through the door's vertical planks.

"Son of a *bitch*!" a man yelped on the other side of the door, which closed until it hit something, and bounced back against the wall.

Seeing more hatted shadows running toward him from the other side of the jailhouse, Hawk ran straight back toward the woodpile and the privy. Behind him, men shouted. Gunfire blasted, slugs singing around him and thudding dully into the ground behind his boots.

Holding his stiffening left arm before his belly and carrying the Henry in his right hand, Hawk ran past the privy, wove through a few spindly cottonwoods, then turned right beyond a vacant corral.

Cows mooed and kicked wood inside the connecting stable.

Hawk dropped into a shallow dry wash, ran several yards down the wash, hopscotching stones to which the snow had not yet clung, then bounded up the opposite bank. In wild currant shrubs, he paused on his haunches, looking around. Beyond was a narrow cut with steep, shale sides. About fifty yards to the right were several cabins with privies and stables, a few small barns and sluice boxes. A few of the cabins spilled light from their windows, vague smudges in the quickly descending night.

Behind Hawk, boots thudded and men shouted angrily. A pistol popped.

"It's a cat, you stupid son of a bitch!"

The sounds grew closer.

Hawk leapt forward, jumping the cut and bulling through the shrubs on the other side. He ran forward blindly, holding the rifle up to shield his face from damp, thorny branches.

Suddenly, the ground fell away beneath his boots. He hit a downgrade on his knees and, instinctively clutching the Henry's breech, turned two violent somersaults as he headed straight down the drop-off.

He glanced off a shrub, rolled, clipped another bush, then turned another couple of somersaults before his back slammed level ground and he lay still.

His gut continued turning somersaults as he blinked his eyes, tried hard to keep them open.

Finally, the lids stayed up, faint fireworks exploding against the violet sky from which big, downy snowflakes slanted. His arm thudded painfully. A heavy, thick wetness was growing under the sleeve of his buckskin, making him shudder from a fleeting, penetrating chill.

He couldn't stay here. The gunmen were too close. If he didn't do something fast, he was liable to pass out and freeze to death.

Grunting and snarling against his inertia, he rose onto his right elbow, looked around. His rifle and hat lay on the far side of the sandy streambed. He gained his hands and knees, a little surprised that nothing felt broken, no organs knocked askew.

He crawled across the high-sided bed, slapped snow from his hat, and donned it. He grabbed the Henry, wiped the grit and snow from the barrel, then tried to stand. He groaned and dropped to his knees.

Nausea washed over him, the ground spinning beneath his boots. The fall and loss of blood had weakened him.

He took the Henry in his left hand and, breathing through pain-gritted teeth, crawled forward, using both knees and only his right hand. He'd crawled only a few yards before the streambed widened and a notch cave opened on his right, about a foot up from the bed.

He stopped, scrutinized the long, narrow cleft. Inside, no shadows moved. Not wanting to risk tussling with a cougar or a wolf, though he doubted either would be holing up this close to the settlement, he grabbed a stick and tossed it into the cave.

When nothing came out, Hawk crawled inside and lay on his right shoulder, facing the streambed. He held his rifle lengthwise along his body, clutching the barrel with his left hand.

He could feel the blood trickling from the wound about six inches up from his elbow. Soon, he'd have to tend it. But now, hearing distant voices, he had to lay as still as possible and hope the killers didn't see where Hawk had tumbled into the streambed. With the snow falling thicker and faster, it wouldn't be long till his tracks would be covered.

But it was too much to hope for.

A minute later, a man's voice rose behind him. "Over this way! I got sign!"

Another minute, and several sets of boots scuffed along the streambed, spurs chinging softly. Men breathed sharply.

"Come out, come out wherever you are!" a man squealed with drunken, devilish glee.

Hawk winced and shoved himself as far back in the notch as he could get, but it wasn't far. The gap was only about three feet wide. By the sounds, the outlaws were heading his way. They'd sure as hell see the cave, and they were certain-sure to check it out.

Hawk scraped a deep breath and slowly, quietly levered a fresh shell into the Henry's chamber.

They'd find him.

But at least a couple were going to wish they hadn't.

11.

ON THE RUN

A voice rose somewhere above and ahead of Hawk. "You, in the streambed—name yourselves!"

"Who the fuck you think it is?" replied a man downstream from Hawk. Someone else laughed.

"Moran, you see sign down there?" asked the man on the ridge over the wash.

"Why do you think we're down here?"

"Well, be quick about finding that bastard. It's gonna be pitch black out here soon, and the wind's pickin' up. La Salle took a bullet, and he's ragin' like a bull buff with its tail on fire. He wants that sumbitch's *head*!"

"Well, if you'd shut up, Tyrell, we might be able to find him!"

A muffled, disgusted curse sounded downstream.

Footsteps approached the cave. Gideon drew his feet in as far as he could, until his heels were pressed against the back wall.

Looking down toward his boots, he saw that the hole continued back behind the embankment. As the sound of boot scrapes and spur chings grew louder, he used his right arm and his legs to scuttle straight down into the stone sheath.

He had the lower half of his body inside the hole when his hat raked off. He reached up to retrieve it, then wiggled as far as he could into the crevice, with a six- or seven-inch stone partition shielding him from the streambed.

"Listen!" someone said only a few feet away.

Silence.

"I heard somethin'."

Hawk held himself still, breathing quietly through parted lips.

"Where do the tracks go?"

"I can't see shit. It's gettin' too dark and the snow's comin' too damn hard."

"Look there."

Silence.

Boots crunched snow. Raspy breathing sounded just beyond Hawk's cramped hideaway.

"Hey, drygulchin' bastard, you in there?"

Three shots sounded in quick succession, the slugs drilling the cleft above Hawk's head, where his entire body had been lying only a minute ago.

Rock shards ticked off his hat and peppered his face. The concussions rang his ears.

Another shot sounded, the slug ricocheting with a twanging whine.

Footsteps grew louder, stopping only a few feet away. Hawk lifted his chin to peer into the cleft he'd just abandoned.

Outside, a shadow moved. A man bent down to peer into the notch—a shaggy-headed hombre with a hat cord swinging beneath his chin. Hawk gritted his teeth, hoping the outlaw didn't inspect the cave's walls too carefully.

The man stood there, one hand resting on the ledge over the notch, for several seconds, his boot making faint squeaking sounds in the snow and gravel as he shifted his weight. His breathing was harsh, frustrated. He dropped the hand from the lip, straightened, and turned away.

"Nothin'."

Someone cursed. The footsteps resumed, then faded as the silhouettes of the five men disappeared up the wash.

Hawk heaved a deep sigh. His muscles relaxed—all but those in his wounded arm. The muscles there seemed to tighten around the bullet hole, making his hand tingle from a pinched blood supply.

He waited for ten minutes, then began to struggle out of the notch. Outside, a horse nickered. Hoof-beats sounded.

"Shit," Hawk muttered, using his right elbow to push his body back into the cleft.

The killers must have decided this was the only place he could be, and they were returning to give the cave a more thorough scrutiny. Hawk wrapped both hands around the Henry and started sliding it slowly up his body, quietly positioning himself for firing.

The hoof falls grew louder until the horse was blowing and snorting just outside the cleft.

"You in the cave . . ." It was a young woman's Southern-accented voice. "The gunmen are gone. It's safe to come out."

Hawk remained still, squeezing the rifle, his heart thudding. Before the cave, the horse stomped around the wash, small sage shrubs snapping beneath its hooves.

"Pssst," the woman said. "Climb on outta there before you freeze to death!"

Hawk's heart slowed slightly. It could be a trap. La Salle had a woman traveling with him. Something told him, however, that this woman wasn't Babe Mayberry.

He struggled out of the hole, poked his head out of the cleft. The woman was a vague shape in a heavy wool coat, sitting the cracked leather saddle of a raw-boned dun. A broad-brimmed man's hat concealed her face. She stared at him for a moment, her shoulders tensing slightly, as though she'd expected to see someone else.

"Come on." She extended a gloved hand toward him. "Climb up behind me, and I'll get you someplace warm!" She paused, saw him hesitate. "I'm Jesse Haskell—Wick's wife."

"What're you doing out here?"

"I heard the shooting. Hurry!"

"You want nothing to do with me, miss. Best ride on."

"You're in no condition to continue tangling with that bunch. Not until that arm's been tended. Now, will you come on?"

Favoring his right arm, Hawk straightened his soupy knees, and looked both ways along the wash. The snow continued falling, a gauzy gray darkness descending fast. The wind blew against him, sending a chill through his bloody arm.

He shuddered.

"Hand me your rifle and climb aboard," the woman urged, her voice impatient, as she slipped her left foot from the stirrup.

Moving toward the horse, careful not to fall, Hawk extended the rifle. The woman took it.

Hawk grabbed the saddle's cantle with his right hand, poked his left foot into the empty stirrup, and swung onto the dun's rump. The horse jumped at the additional weight and crabbed around, nickering. Hawk took his rifle back from the woman, grabbed the slack of her coat with his right hand, and laid the rifle across the cantle between them.

"Oh, hush, Ed," the woman admonished, neck-reining the horse around and clucking it up the wash.

When they'd followed a trail out of the wash and were moving on a two-track trail past several dark cabins huddled along the wash, Hawk cleared his throat. "How'd you know I was there?"

"I seen you fallin' down the bank. That was quite a tumble. I was gonna ride down and see if you were all right, but then I seen the gunmen, decided to hole up on the other ridge. I'm powerful glad they didn't see me."

"Thanks for the help," Hawk said.

"You hit?"

"Just a flesh wound, I think."

"I'll tend it for you. I've done a lot of tending and mending around here, on account of our doctor's foggy on opium most of the time."

The woman didn't say anything else until they'd passed two lit cabins and turned west down a slight grade, toward another ravine. "Who are you, anyway, if you don't mind me askin'?"

"Hollis is the name." Hawk paused. "Who did you think I was?"

"I thought you were one of Wick's deputies. I seen you shooting at those men by the jailhouse, decided to follow as close as I dared till you got shed of 'em. You don't know what become of the deputies, do you—Rose an' them?"

"I saw one deputy dead inside the jailhouse."

Saying nothing, the young woman swung the horse up to the door of a squat, gray barn snugged against a low rimrock. She swung her right foot over the horn, slid easily out of the saddle, then reached up to help Hawk down.

"How many men are there?" she asked darkly.

Hawk shook his head. "Upwards of twenty. I mighta dispatched a couple."

When he had both feet on the ground, she moved to his right arm and led him around the barn and small corral toward a two-story clapboard house, painted white, with a stone fireplace. There was a picket fence around the yard, and when she opened the gate, Hawk saw a snow-dusted brick walk leading across the yard to the house's front porch.

A couple of spindly transplanted trees stood in the yard, and a row of dried-up, snow-sodden flowers drooped along the porch's stone foundation. To the left lay the remains of a small kitchen garden, with yellow squash vines, and a few desiccated corn stalks slumped at the far end.

On the wind, Hawk smelled pine smoke.

Mrs. Haskell opened the porch's screen door, stepped back, and held it for him as he mounted the three brick steps. He stopped on the porch, where the hybrid smell of dirt, potatoes, gourds, and molasses hung heavy in the cold, still air. She let the screen door slam shut, hooked it, then moved around him and opened the main door to the house.

Hawk stepped into a lamplit, wooden-floored kitchen, the boards slightly uneven but well-scrubbed. Warm air pushed luxuriantly against him, his eyes stinging a little from the smoke. The air was moist from the steam swirling up from a big, copper boiler chugging on the kitchen's black iron range. The steam smelled of eucalyptus leaves.

Another iron pot dribbled meat juice down its sides, adding the smell of venison stew to the pot-pourri of aromas. On a shelf over the stove sat three bread loaves, the oily brown crusts glistening in the lamplight.

To his right, beyond a scrubbed wooden table, the fire popped and snapped in the fireplace. A young girl, maybe thirteen or fourteen, stood before the hearth, holding a bundle of quilts in which, he assumed, nestled an infant. The girl wore a quilted black and white shirt, patched blue jeans, and high, fur-trimmed moccasins. Her tangled brown hair hung straight down past her shoulders, giving her a half-feral look.

As she rocked the infant gently in her cradled arms, shifting her weight between her hips, she regarded Hawk with wary curiosity in her wide, brown eyes.

Mrs. Haskell slid a chair out from the end of the table. "Sit here, Mr. Howell, and I'll tend that arm for you."

Hawk leaned the rifle against the wall, within easy reach, and slumped into the chair. The girl holding the child continued staring at him. To put her at ease, he turned up the corners of his mouth briefly. Her expression didn't change, and she didn't turn away.

"That's Claudelle, my little sister," said Mrs. Haskell. "She can't talk. The little one's Romey, my son—Wick's and mine. He has a cough. That's why I'm steaming the house."

She was unbuttoning her bulky blanket coat as she stood before him, her cheeks flushed from the cold. She appeared in her early twenties, a pretty, outdoors-seasoned woman with bright, hazel eyes and wide, expressive mouth.

She hung her wet coat on a hook by the stove.

"When I heard the shootin', I saddled Ed and rode up toward Main Street to see what was happening." She knelt before Hawk, her cheeks drawn, eyes wide with fear. "It's La Salle, isn't it? He's here to kill Wick."

Hawk looked at the girl. She jostled the infant automatically, returning Hawk's stare with an anxious one of her own.

Turning back to Haskell's young wife, Hawk said, "I'm afraid so."

Mrs. Haskell dropped her eyes to the floor between Hawk's wet boots. Her shoulders slumped. "When I heard the shootin', I knew it was them. I've been waitin' for 'em ever since Wick brought in that Bob." Her mouth pinched when she said the name of La Salle's younger brother. Her lips quivered slightly. "Now they're here."

"I don't intend to let them kill your husband, Mrs. Haskell."

She lifted her eyes to his. "Are you a lawman?"

"That's right."

"You're here to help Wick?"

Hawk nodded.

She squinted at him, eyes shaded by the hat she still wore. "Just one man?"

"Sometimes one man can be more effective than a whole army," Hawk said, wincing when pain shot up his arm. "Though I reckon I haven't exactly proven it so far. . . ."

"Take your coat off," she said, rising. "I'll take a look at that wound."

12.

MRS. HASKELL

AS Jesse Haskell went to the kitchen sink and pumped water into a porcelain washbasin, Hawk stood and unbuttoned his coat, keeping an eye on the first story's four windows. If the killers tracked him and Mrs. Haskell here, not only would Hawk be trapped, but three innocent people would be trapped, as well.

When he'd wrestled out of the damp coat with its bloody left sleeve, the woman set the washbasin, a half-full whiskey bottle, and what looked like a sewing kit on the table. She took Hawk's coat, hauled a rocking chair near the fire, and draped the coat over the rocker's back.

The woman checked on the baby in Claudelle's arms, muttered something to the girl that Hawk couldn't hear, then returned to the kitchen. She sat down in the chair near Hawk, removed her hat, and tossed it onto the table. Hawk watched her blond hair spill down around her shoulders, mesmerized, his heart hammering his breastbone. "Linda."

As she opened the sewing kit, she glanced at him, then turned away. She looked at him again, frowning.

"My name's Jesse."

Her voice came to him as if from down a deep hole. The rushing in his ears abated. "What?"

"You called me Linda." She stared at him skeptically, then stuck her hand into the sewing kit, removed several strips of cloth and a scissors. "Give me your hand."

Hawk lifted his left hand from his lap, supporting the elbow with his right, extended it over the table. "What did I call you?"

"Linda."

Hawk felt his face burn, felt his insides tighten. He hadn't heard anyone else utter the name in a long time. "Sorry, I . . ." Not knowing what else to say, he let the sentence die unfinished.

Jesse took the scissors and, holding Hawk's wrist with one hand, began cutting straight up the sleeve with the other. Hawk couldn't help staring at her wide-set eyes, the several freckles on her pale cheeks, the rich, golden hair swirling about her shoulders. She was Linda's size, too—about five-two or -three. Slender. She had the slight look of a tomboy, which Linda had had before Jubal's birth and all the worries that had come with the raising of a slow, sensitive child.

Jesse Haskell glanced at him, saw him staring, and flushed.

"Who's Linda?" she asked.

The question jolted him out of his reverie. "My wife." Before she could ask anything else, he asked a question of his own, more to steer the conversation away from Linda than anything else. "How long have you and Sheriff Haskell been married?"

"Three years next April." She'd cut the sleeve away and had leaned over to scrutinize the bloody hole in Hawk's arm, just up from the elbow. She twisted the arm slightly as she lowered her head to peer at the other side. She touched her finger to the edge of the hole, pressed down slightly, squinting. Her soft, warm breath puffed against his skin. "Looks like it went all the way through. Hurt much?"

"I've had worse."

"Don't think it hit the bone. I'm not gonna stitch. Needs to breathe. It'll mend as long as you keep it clean."

She released the arm and uncorked the whiskey bottle. Hawk held the wound over the basin, set his teeth as she splashed a good dollop of the whiskey over the bloody hole. The burn seared him deep but his face remained stoic, brows ridged over eyes set deep in dark sockets. She turned his arm over and splashed more whiskey over the exit hole.

"How did you know La Salle was coming?" she asked as she balled a strip of cloth in her hand, dipped it in the water.

"I tracked him here."

"From where?"

"The mountains."

She glanced at him, her eyes worried, as she scrubbed gently at the blood along the ragged edges of the entrance hole. "Wick'll be headin' back to town tomorrow."

"By the time he gets here, La Salle's gang will be . . . gone."

"I was figurin' to ride out, try to get word to him—"

Hawk placed his hand on hers. His voice was firm. "It's blowing up bad out there. You'll never make it. Give me time to handle these men."

"You mean, arrest them?"

Hawk looked away. "Handle them."

She stared at him for a long time, the bridge of her nose wrinkling. She squeezed the bloody cloth out in the basin, and said softly, "You sure you're a law-man?" She glanced down at the badge on his shirt.

When he did not respond, she continued cleaning the wound. "Wick's a good man," she said pensively. "He's twelve years older than me, but when my pa died in his mine, Wick took both me and Claudelle under his wing. I was . . . workin' at the time." She glanced at him demurely. "Over to the Venus."

"We've all done things we regret."

While she dressed his arm, her fingers feeling good against his skin, he sat enjoying the warmth and the peace and quiet of the neat little house. The water bubbled on the stove. The fireplace popped and siz-zled with bleeding pine resin. Outside, the wind moaned under the eaves, the snow lashed the walls and windows.

When the baby had gone to sleep, the girl laid him in the cradle to the right of the fire. She sat on the floor and rocked the cradle with her foot while she sewed beads into a deer-hide knife sheath. Occasionally, she looked up, swiping her hair from her face with the back of a hand, and looked at Hawk, as if making sure he was still in the same place. She sniffed, ran the heel of her hand across her nose, then returned her attention to the sheath.

When Jesse had finished cleaning and wrapping the wound, she told Claudelle to fetch one of Haskell's shirts from upstairs. As the girl stood and opened the door to the enclosed stairway, the stale, cold upstairs air wafting against Hawk, Jesse opened the kitchen door, and tossed out the bloody water.

"I'll make coffee and have supper on the table in a few minutes," she told Hawk.

"No need for that." Hawk pushed himself to his feet. "When your sister brings the shirt, I'll be on my way."

"No," she said, turning to him sharply. He could read her thoughts. While she wanted the men who threatened her husband taken care of, she didn't want to be alone with her worries. "You've lost blood. Best eat before you can face the cold again."

Hawk considered it. The night was still early. He might have better luck at the Venus later on, when La Salle's men had had time to oil their tonsils and dull their reactions with tarantula juice. Later, Hawk could just stroll through the front door and start shooting, take care of the nasty business in a few minutes.

He was joshing himself.

Truth was, he wanted to stay here for a while, bask in the warmth and the companionship of a woman who reminded him of Linda and of his own tidy home back in Dakota.

Six days after leaving Pagosa Springs, Luke Morgan sniffed out the trail of Gideon Hawk.

With the help of others he met along the trail and who'd seen a man who'd fit Hawk's description—a snake-oil drummer in a gaudily painted wagon, two down-at-heels drovers, and a traveling acting troupe—he managed to stay on it. On his eighth day out, and just when he was closing on his quarry, the snow began to fall.

It fell so hard that, under any other circumstances, Morgan would have looked for shelter. Refusing to give up, he rode on.

The snow got thicker as the sun went down. The wind blew it hard against his face. His damp trousers froze against his legs and, later, his butt and legs froze to his saddle.

But the drovers he'd run into that morning said there was a town out here. Hawk was headed for it, Morgan knew. Because the men he was trailing were headed for it.

Which meant Morgan was headed for it, too. He

wouldn't stop until he got there and drilled a bullet through Hawk's twisted brain.

He gave the horse its head. The trail was no longer visible through the high, rolling desert stippled with sage and rabbit brush and occasional boulders strewn like some giant's dice, but the horse would follow it. The horse could probably smell the town, the luxurious aroma of warm stables and fresh hay. . . .

Morgan dozed in the saddle.

He wasn't aware of the horse leaving the main trail and following a secondary wagon track onto a low mountain shoulder. He was, however vaguely, aware of a distant horse's whinny beneath the wind and snow rushing against him.

Wood smoke teased his nostrils, tossed about by the storm.

Lifting his head, he opened his eyes, the lids frozen to his face. Through ice-fringed lashes, he saw a low cabin huddled against boulders strewn beneath the lip of an overarching ridge. Light from two sashed windows cast a dim light on the storm.

The door opened and a tall, stooped man stepped out. He had a pipe in his mouth, a shotgun in his hands.

"Go on, drift!" he yelled around the pipe as he moved through the whistling wind toward Morgan. He wore a cloth, leather-billed cap. "Keep your trouble down yonder! Me, I'm havin' a right fine time up here *alone*!"

Morgan's right hand slid toward the pistol on his right hip.

"Goddamn you!" yelled the man moving toward

him, cheeked up to his Greener's butt. "Say hello to your Maker!"

Before Morgan could lift his frozen coat from his pistol butt, the shotgun exploded.

When he'd donned Wick Haskell's shirt, only a little tight in the chest and a half inch short in the sleeves, and while the women prepared the supper, Hawk strolled into the living room to look out the window on the south side of the house. Night had fallen and the snow continued to tick against the windows.

As he turned to look out the opposite window, he let his eyes linger across the tintypes on the fireplace mantle.

There were two pictures of Jesse, in a simple but formal gown, and a handsome, sandy-haired man with a dragoon mustache and a crisp bowler hat. Wick Haskell. There was another of Jesse, Haskell, and Claudelle, whose hair was neatly brushed and who wore a frilly white dress and held a bouquet of wildflowers in her hands. Jesse was holding the baby, whose eyes were pinched shut, a small, white, lace-edged cap snugged on his tiny head.

On the wall beside the north window was a piece of framed embroidery into the middle of which a verse had been stitched:

> *O God, our help in ages past,*
> *Our hope for years to come,*
> *Our shelter from the stormy blast,*
> *And our eternal home.*

"Supper's ready, Mr. Howell," Jesse said, setting a plate of thick, crusty bread on the table.

As Hawk and Claudelle took their seats at the table, Jesse went into the living room to nurse the baby, which had started to fuss. She rocked and hummed softly in the rocking chair, turned toward the fire. When she finished, she returned the sleeping baby to its cradle, and sat down at the table to Hawk's left.

They ate in silence, the wind and snow blowing against the house, the baby fussing quietly in the other room before drifting back to sleep. The fireplace popped and hissed, logs shifting with soft thuds. The broiler bubbled atop the range, and the lanterns guttered with the drafts.

While Hawk ate, shoving the rich, meaty stew onto his fork with a hunk of the buttered bread, he remembered other meals like this, on stormy nights like this, in his own house, with his own family.

A hundred years ago, it seemed to him now.

At the same time, only yesterday . . .

"Thanks for the supper," he said when his plate was clean, scraping his chair back. "It hit the spot."

Jesse and Claudelle regarded him anxiously.

"What are you going to do?" Jesse asked, frowning.

"I reckon I'll figure that out as I go."

"But it's storming. And there's twenty of them. . . ."

Hawk retrieved his coat from the rocker. It was dry and a bit stiff, almost hot. He shrugged into it as he moved back toward the door.

"By now, they probably think I'm dead in the snowy brush," Hawk said, buttoning the coat. "That means I have surprise on my side."

He donned his hat and picked up his rifle, nodded to both women looking up at him from the table. "Good night. Thanks again." He stared at Jesse, his eyes glinting darkly. "Don't worry."

He hefted his rifle and opened the door.

Jesse had stood, and now she followed him across the porch. She watched as, hunkered down inside his coat, he trotted off toward the stable, the snow and the windy night quickly engulfing him, his boot tracks filling in behind him.

She turned, hooked the porch door, and walked back inside. When she'd closed the inside door and locked it, she realized that Claudelle was staring at her, grunting to get her attention.

Jesse looked at her sister. Claudelle had pulled a magazine off the pile stacked to her right. She extended it toward Jesse, shaking it with one hand and poking a finger at the story it was turned to.

Jesse dropped her gaze to the magazine.

Across the top of the page stretched the story's title in thick, black letters:

THE TALE OF THE ROGUE LAWMAN

13.

"THANK GOD YOU CAME
BACK . . . MR. HAWK"

"I want that son of a bitch's *head*!" Ed La Salle shouted, grabbing his sister's wrist in which she clenched a rag soaked with her brother's blood.

"So you said," Babe said with strained tolerance. "And you're gonna have it, Ed. But if you don't let me finish cleanin' that cut, you're gonna bleed dry!"

Ed cursed and released his sister's hand. Babe continued cleaning the cut, dipping the rag into the washbasin sitting on the table before them. La Salle leaned forward, resting his forearms on the tabletop, a water glass half-filled with whiskey standing between his wrists.

He dropped his head toward the glass, so that Babe could reach the long furrow that Hawk's bullet had carved across the top of La Salle's head, from his right temple to the bald spot at the crown. His hat sat on the chair beside him, a hole in both the front and back of the crown, just above the brim.

Several of his riders stood around, watching Babe work. All the men had been called downstairs, and the entire gang, except for the men Hawk had either killed or wounded, or those out still searching for the shooter, were gathered around the table. Some sat, others stood, watching the blood run in several rivulets down La Salle's bearded face.

Bigwater Nils Freedman was rolling a cigarette. "You think it coulda been Haskell?"

"That hombre in Tucson told me Haskell was average height. Had sandy hair kinda long, and always wore a brown, bullet-crowned sombrero." La Salle winced as his sister dabbed at the cut. "This son of a bitch was tall. Had dark hair. And he was wearin' a flat-brimmed, black hat."

"It was pretty dark out there, Ed," Babe said.

"Wasn't that dark."

Boots and voices sounded outside. La Salle frowned as he turned his pain-dark eyes to the front of the saloon, where the inside doors had been closed and locked over the batwings. The shade had been drawn over the big window. Someone pounded one of the doors.

"Open up, it's Bergstrom."

"Let 'em in, Dave," La Salle yelled to the man who'd been standing near the front.

The men around La Salle turned as six men

shrouded in snow and frost came in on a blast of cold air and snow, beating their hats against their thighs and stomping snow from their boots. The draft made the fire spit and chug.

"Close the damn doors," Babe yelled. "You're let-tin' the warm air out!"

One of the six closed the doors while the others strode up to La Salle's table, the other men around the table making way.

"Did you find the son of a bitch?" La Salle asked.

"Didn't find him, Ed," said Jabber Faraday, whose beard was frosted white, his cheeks apple red. He grabbed the drink out of another man's hand, tossed it back, wiped his mouth with the back of the hand holding the glass. "Seen plenty of blood in the snow, though."

"I think he crawled into some brush and died," said a short, scrawny rider, the oldest of the bunch at fifty-three, named Matt "Stovepipe" Green. He wore a necklace of dried Apache ears around his neck, and he adjusted them now as he opened his antelope-hide coat. "I gotta pretty good feelin' I lung-shot him."

"Your eyes have gone to hell, Stovepipe," scoffed La Salle. "Shit, they were goin' to hell back when you and me were market huntin'. How would you know you even *hit* him?"

"How many fingers am I holdin' up?" asked a man across the table from Stovepipe.

Stovepipe glowered at him.

"Enough o' this bullshit," said Babe. "We need to figure out what we're gonna do about this hombre that killed four of us and wounded four more, includin' *Ed*!"

"I think it's Haskell," said Faraday, pouring himself a drink at the bar. "I think he seen the storm comin', rode back to town early, and sniffed out the smell o' his own death, if'n you get my drift." He winked, threw back half a glass of whiskey, and choked. "Hell, who else could it be?"

"Maybe he took a likin' to black hats, Ed," said Babe, pouring whiskey over the rag she was using to clean Ed's head.

"I reckon it's worth lookin' into," Ed said, cursing as Babe dabbed at his head with the alcohol-drenched cloth. He looked at the bartender, whom Ed, when the shooting had broken out, had ordered tied to a chair in front of a *ristra*-bedecked ceiling joist. "You, big man, where's Haskell live?"

The barman just glowered at him, his bull neck turning red.

"Stovepipe," La Salle said mildly, "the big man must not have heard me. Maybe you could see to cleanin' out his ears with your bowie knife."

After leaving the Haskell house, Hawk hunkered down behind the black hulk of an empty cabin, the wind whistling in the chimney and knocking the broken door against its frame. Snow lashed against him, a gust so thick he couldn't see but a few feet before his face.

Then it lightened, as if taking a breath, and he looked around, not sure where he was. When he'd climbed out of the ravine, he'd thought he was heading east toward the hotel, but all he could see ahead was a fold of low, rocky hills.

He must've gotten turned around.

He moved around the cabin, regained his bearings, and as a fresh gust lashed him and nearly blew his hat off his head, jogged past a chicken coop, a stable, and a cabin in which a silhouetted face appeared. As Hawk dashed past the window, the face vanished. A moment later, the light went out.

The tall backsides of the Main Street buildings had come together before him when he spotted boot tracks in the drifting snow. Four sets spaced about four feet apart. They trailed off between a knoll and a large woodpile, heading south, back the way Hawk had just come.

Back toward the ravine and the Haskell place.

Even as Hawk stared at the blue-black indentations, his stomach tightening, his gloved fingers squeezing his rifle, their edges dissolved under the wind's eroding lash.

Hawk turned and followed the tracks, the drifting snow licking nearly to his knees in some places. He followed the tracks up the brushy hills, into a cut, across a bridge, and over the shoulder of a low rimrock. He stopped at the top of the shoulder, a hard knot in his stomach.

The tracks turned at the bottom of the shoulder and angled toward the lamplit Haskell house.

As Hawk bolted forward and began running down the hill, he thought he heard a shrill, muffled scream

on the wind. He leapt drifts and snow-mounded
stones and sage tufts, approached the house, and sidled up to a window in the north wall.

Inside, the baby cried. Men's voices rose.

Hawk turned to the window and spit a curse into
the wind. Frost covered the glass. All he could see
were moving shadows and guttering lamplight.

He ran around the house and approached the front
door, crouched over his rifle and ducking his head as
he passed a window. They hadn't planted a man outside. He mounted the porch steps, drew the porch
door wide, stepped softly across the porch to the
front door.

The voices rose clearly now—one man doing
most of the talking. Boots pounded the wooden
floors upstairs and down. The baby cried shrilly. A
woman sobbed.

Hawk peered through the door glass. Four people
were in the living room—two men and Jesse and
Claudelle. One of the men was bear-hugging
Claudelle from behind, lifting the girl several feet off
the floor, pinning her arms to her sides. She kicked
her feet and shook her head wildly, grunting and
yelling, her tangled hair whipping.

Jesse was on the floor, running her right hand
across her mouth and looking up at the second man
standing beside the baby's cradle. The brass casing
of his long-barreled Navy Colt flashed in the firelight. In his other hand he held one of the bloody
cloths Jesse had used to clean Hawk's wound, an end
dangling toward the split-pine floor.

Hawk set his left hand on the doorknob, was about to turn it when boots thundered, shaking the house. Hawk's hand froze on the knob. Two men entered the room through the stairway door, one behind the other, both holding Winchesters.

"No sign of him upstairs," said an unshaven gent in a soggy blanket coat.

The man by the cradle tossed the bloody cloth at Jesse and pointed his gun at the baby, clicking the hammer back. "Where'd he go?"

Hawk threw the door wide and stepped into the room. "You boys looking for me?"

They all jerked their faces at him, eyes snapping wide. Hawk recognized the man with the pistol aimed at the crying baby as Casey Coyle, an outlaw he'd once lost in the Turtle Mountains of northern Dakota.

Coyle swung his pistol at Hawk, who triggered the Henry from his shoulder, drilling the .44 round through the right center of Coyle's chest. Coyle fired the Navy into the floor three feet from Hawk's left boot, and stumbled back against the wall, raging.

Hawk ejected the spent casing and swung the Henry left, where the two men who'd been upstairs were pivoting toward him, raising their Winchesters. They were moving at roughly the same speed.

Hawk shot the man on the right first, the one on the left second.

Both stumbled back, clutching their fatal wounds. The man on the right knocked over the baby's cradle, the blanket-wrapped little bundle spilling out of the

box and rolling against the wall. The man fell atop
the cradle, smashing it flat as death spasms wracked
his legs and thrashed his arms.

In the corner of his right eye, Hawk saw the fourth
man drop Claudelle, shove her brusquely forward,
and reach across his waist for the revolver holstered
butt-forward on his left hip. Hawk threw himself
straight back as the gun exploded, the bullet missing
by an eyelash and barking into a cupboard.

Sliding across the floor on his butt, Hawk raised
the Henry and fired. His bullet slammed into an unlit
bracket lamp three inches right of the man's head.
The man ducked and winced, glanced at the shattered
lamp, then grinned as he turned to Hawk, showing
several silver teeth.

He thumbed back his Colt's hammer, took two
lumbering strides straight forward, stopped, and extended the revolver straight out from his shoulder.

As Hawk levered another shell, his chest grew
tight. The man had the drop on him. As the ejected
shell casing arced, smoking, over Hawk's right
shoulder, Claudelle climbed to her knees, screaming
shrilly and throwing the fireplace poker. It slammed
into the man's extended arm at the same moment the
revolver discharged.

The bullet nipped the sole of Hawk's right boot
and barked into the floor.

"You little whore!" the gunman raged, stumbling
over a footstool, then turning toward Claudelle.

As he began to raise his cocked revolver at the
girl, Jesse screamed, *"No!"*

Hawk's rifle drowned out her voice. A small round hole appeared in the man's left temple. His head tipped toward his right shoulder, as if he'd been slapped.

Both arms fell slack. He staggered, turned toward Hawk, blinking groggily, eyes vaguely befuddled. He froze. His eyes rolled back in his head. He dropped to his knees; then his face hit the floor.

He sighed and broke wind, and then he was dead.

Claudelle bounded toward the man, dropped to her knees beside him, and, screaming, pounded his back with her fists. Jesse stooped, gently scooped the baby off the floor. Hawk was relieved to see the little bundle moving around inside its blankets.

He stood. "The child all right?"

Cooing to the screaming baby, rocking it gently, Jesse moved toward Hawk. "He's fine." Her voice was pinched with fear. "Thank God you came back . . . Mr. Hawk."

Hawk's brow furrowed. He followed Jesse's glance to the table, where the magazine lay open to the story about the Rogue Lawman. He exhaled sharply as he turned and went outside. On the front stoop, he peered into the storm.

Seeing no other gunmen, he moved back inside, shut the door, and threw the bolt.

Claudelle knelt beside the dead man, a pool of thick blood growing around his head. She wasn't beating him anymore. She sat back on her heels, head down, sobbing quietly.

The baby bawled in Jesse's arms. Its mother studied Hawk with trepidation.

Fear trilled her voice. "What do we do now? The others will come."

Hawk laid his rifle on the table, walked over to Claudelle, stooped down, and gently helped her stand. He led her over to the table, pulled a chair out, and eased her into it. She buried her face in her arms, sobbing. Hawk smoothed her hair gently and turned to Jesse.

She stared at him with a puzzled frown.

"You have any neighbors?" Hawk asked.

"None close. And none friendly."

"Why's that?"

"Very few people in Skinners' Bottoms wanted Wick to bring Little Bob to justice . . . over a couple of Mexican girls. They were afraid what La Salle would do to the town."

"Figures." Hawk looked around the two rooms. "This place have a cellar you can hide in?"

Jesse stomped her right foot, the boot heel making a hollow thump on the boards. "Under the kitchen. But it's too cold for the baby."

Hawk considered the problem. The cellar might not work for hiding the women, but it would do just fine for hiding the four dead men. When he'd lifted the rug and the cellar door, he dumped each of the four bodies into the hole.

"Rifle?"

Jesse nodded. The baby sleeping in her arms, she stood watching him from near the table. Claudelle regarded him with grim fascination, her face streaked with tears, strands of hair pasted to it.

"Get it, then blow out the lamps. Keep the fire low. Not that it'll do much good, but keep the door locked." He picked up his Henry and headed for the door.

"What're you going to do?"

"Keep La Salle too distracted to come looking for the men in your cellar."

He turned the doorknob. She placed a hand on his arm, stopping him. "Is the story true? Did you really lose your wife and your little boy?"

Hawk looked at her, his eyes deeply shadowed below his hat brim, his brow ridged. "I didn't lose them. They were murdered." He twisted the knob, went out, and closed the door behind him.

Holding the baby in one arm, Jesse bolted the door. She turned her back to it and stood frozen, hearing Hawk's boots thump across the porch and crunch the snow briefly before the wind swallowed them.

14.

DUNKLEE AND JENSEN

A harsh, grating voice woke Luke Morgan from a deep sleep. "Stinkin' dog livers—there you go again! Don't tell me that ace came from the deck. You slipped it outta your sleeve. I *seen* you!"

Morgan opened his eyes, stared up at a low, timbered ceiling. His head throbbed painfully. His limbs felt heavy and spongy. Each eyelid was a pound of butter.

He wanted to go back to sleep, but he couldn't figure out where he was, or to whom the voice belonged.

"I told you what was gonna happen next time you cheated at poker, Jensen. Don't go sayin' you wasn't warned."

Morgan turned his head to the side. Across the small, cramped room was a table where two men sat, playing cards spread on the table before them. The man on the right—tall and leathery, with thin hair swept straight back from a pronounced widow's peak, and a long, aquiline nose—slid his chair back and pulled an old cap-and-ball pistol from its holster. Thumbing the hammer back, he raised the pistol over the table and a half-empty whiskey bottle, leveled the rusty barrel at the man sitting across from him.

Unless Morgan was delusional, it was a human skeleton dressed in a greasy calico shirt, deerskin vest, and snakeskin suspenders holding up a pair of blue cavalry trousers, the cuffs of which were stuffed inside tall, lace-up, hobnailed boots.

The lawman blinked and stared again. Perched atop the skeleton's head was a leather hat, tipped rakishly over one gaping eye socket. Around the bony neck was a red neckerchief with white polka dots.

The skeleton sat with its back against the far wall, quarter-facing the table and the cards spread faceup from the scarred gray surface. A frosty black window shone behind its left shoulder.

"You took my wife, you son of a bitch," said the man across from the skeleton. "And now you take my money!"

He raised the pistol, squinted down the barrel. "Don't make a fool o' yourself, beggin' for your life. It won't do no—"

He stopped when Morgan raised up on one elbow, making the cot creak. The oldster turned, surprise in his drink-bleary eyes, the pistol wilting in his hand.

"Well, look at you. Up and movin' about!"

Morgan remembered the man who'd run out of the cabin, a pipe in his mouth, shotgun in his arms. The last thing he remembered was seeing the shotgun flash, hearing the blast mix with the howling wind that continued to moan outside the cabin's creaky walls. Snow lashed the windows. Morgan's pants were still damp. He touched his hair: dry.

The old man stood, holstered the old cap-and-ball, and squatted down beside Morgan's cot. His eyes were red, his breath fetid from liquor. "Listen, now, I didn't know you was no lawman. I—"

"What happened?"

"I triggered my shotgun into the air to spook you. I figured you were one o' them men raisin' hell down in the town. Your horse was the one that spooked." He chuckled nervously. "It sunfished, plopped ye in the snow. Musta hit your head on a rock. You was out. Your coat came open, and I seen your badge. Can I get you a drink?"

Morgan raked his eyes around the cabin, wincing against the throbbing in his head. In a corner hunkered a small, black stove, stoked till the iron glowed sunset red. It was doing its job. Morgan felt sweat run down his cheeks in spite of the chill lingering deep in his bones.

His coat had been thrown over the back of a hand-hewn chair near the stove. His pistol belt was coiled on the seat, beneath his snuff-colored hat spotted with moisture.

He gently swung his feet to the floor, sat at the end

of the cot, and pressed both hands to his temples. "Where's my horse?"

"Stabled him with my own. Don't worry—I gave him plenty of fresh oats, hay, and water, though as cold as it is, the water's prob'ly froze by now." The man stood, running his hands along his thighs, as if to smooth the wrinkles from his jeans. "Like I said, I didn't know you was—"

"Don't worry, mister. . . ."

"Ezekial Dunklee. My friends call me Zeke."

"That one of your *friends* over there?" Morgan flicked one hand out from his temple, indicating the skeleton in the leather hat and cavalry blues.

Dunklee turned to the skeleton. "How 'bout it, Jensen? You reckon I'm low enough to call a stinky sack of old bones my *friend*? And a cardsharpie to boot!"

Dunklee looked at Morgan. "Reckon he used to be." Dunklee cackled like an old witch. "Hell, I know ole Jensen's dead. I ain't crazy, though some would think so. *Used* to be my minin' partner, till he chipped into a nest of sand rattlers!" The old man slapped his leg and guffawed, increasing the throbs in Morgan's skull. "I keep him sittin' there so I can tongue-lash him for runnin' off with my squaw. The joke was on both of us. Rain Flower ran away from him faster'n she ran away from me, an' ole Jensen came back here with his hat in his hands!"

"I suppose Jensen breaking into the snakes' nest was purely an accident."

The old man snickered. "It'd be kinda hard to

prove otherwise now, wouldn't it?" He splashed whiskey into a tin cup and handed it to Morgan. "Have you a splash o' that. Corn whiskey outta my own tub. Put fur around your eyeballs."

Morgan took the cup and sipped. It burned going down, and twisted his gut, but once it let go it warmed him deeply, eased the pounding in his head. It took him a moment to find his voice. "Where am I, anyway? I must've fallen asleep in the saddle."

The old man had sat back down in his chair, crossed a knee over the other. A short, gray braid, wrapped in rawhide, curled back behind his left ear. "Just north of Skinners' Bottoms. That where you was headed?"

Morgan nodded and took another sip of the coffin varnish. "You mentioned men raising hell in the town."

"Been hearin' shootin' off and on for the past several hours. Want nothin' to do with it. I was here first. The whole town, as fer as I'm concerned, is trespassin' on my claim." He cursed and sipped his whiskey. "Nothin' I can do about it, though, but stay up here and mind my own business, expect them to mind theirs!"

"Did you see these men—these hell-raisers?"

"Don't need to see 'em. I know who they are. The La Salle bunch. Come to take revenge on Sheriff Haskell for hangin' La Salle's brother, Bob." Dunklee chuffed with rancor. "Damn fool. He knew better. Shoulda let Little Bob well enough alone. It ain't like he savaged *white* girls." He looked in his cup, brows angrily furrowed. "What the hell—burn the whole damn town, I say. Give me back my claim." He finished off the cup.

Morgan heaved himself to his feet, staggered a little as he moved to the table.

"You best sit down, Marshal. You're addled a mite."

"Which way's the town?"

"South. Straight out that door and down the hill about two hundred yards."

Morgan set his cup on the table, steadied himself with one hand on the tabletop, then moved to the front door. He opened it, stepped outside.

Dunklee's shrill yell rose behind him. "Holy blazes, lawman. What're you doin'? It's stormin' out there!"

Morgan shut the door behind him and looked around. He could see little but blowing snow and darkness. Ahead and right was a small log stable, the wind piling the snow on its windward side.

He squinted toward the town. Hawk was after the gang. Which meant that Morgan needed only to locate the gang, and he'd locate Hawk, as well.

The only question was, who did he take down first? Hawk, or the men Gideon had been trailing? The only man he had a warrant for was his old colleague. Unless he caught any of the gang breaking the law, Hawk was his primary objective.

There was the problem of the storm, but Morgan doubted Hawk would be hindered by the weather. That meant Morgan couldn't afford to be, either.

Turning, he threw open the cabin door, went back inside. The old man was shoving a split-pine log through the open stove door. Morgan splashed another jigger of whiskey into his cup, threw it back, and reached for his gun belt.

The old man shut the door and latched it, his eyes on Morgan. "Say, what're you up to, lawman?"

"The town's about two hundred yards away, straight down the hill?"

"You ain't goin' down there now, are you? It's a frozen hell out there. You'll catch the chilblains and die in a drift!"

"I got business."

"Those badmen'll be there in the mornin'. *They* ain't crazy enough to go out when the weather's foul! Sit down and have a drink." The old man tossed a hand toward the cards on the table before the skeleton. "Room for more men and more money . . ."

Morgan donned his coat and hat, grabbed his Winchester from the wall right of the door. "Thanks for the drink, Mr. Dunklee. I'll be back in the morning for my horse."

"Suit yourself." Dunklee shrugged as Morgan went out.

Dunklee stared after the lawman. Snow skittered through the opening. The lamps and candles nearly blew out.

The old man spit and slammed the door. He went to the table, refilled his cup from the whiskey bottle. As he lifted the cup to his lips, he glanced at the skeleton. He nodded.

"You're mostly full of dog dung, Jensen, but I reckon this time you're right. That badge-toter's about to meet your pal, the Reaper!"

Crouching low, Hawk ran through the gap between the millinery shop and a drugstore, ducked under a hitch rack, and hunkered down behind a stock trough. Removing his hat and squinting his eyes against the wind-driven snow, he peered over the trough's icy lip at the Venus on the other side of the street.

The upstairs windows were shuttered, but wan lamplight shone through the cracks. Downstairs, shades were drawn over the main window, and the glass doors were shut tight against the storm. Because of the weather, La Salle hadn't posted outside guards. But Hawk would have bet gold against greenbacks that every door was well scrutinized from inside the building.

"Oh, for a two-pounder cannon and a pocketful of grape," he muttered as he turned and began running back between the buildings.

He made a wide arc around the eastern edge of town and came up on the hotel from the alley behind it. He hunkered behind an L-shaped pile of split cordwood, regarded the wooden door barely visible in the darkness below the landing of an outside stairway. Seeing no one at the rear of the building, he ran to the door, slowly turned the knob.

Locked.

He looked up at the floor of the landing ten feet

above. The door at the top of the stairs was probably also locked and guarded. Sometime, however, someone was going to have to come out for wood or to use the privy or to make a quick pass around the building.

Hawk ran back around the woodpile, and brushed out a clear patch of ground, then hunkered down to wait. He crouched low in his coat, occasionally reaching up to rub the feeling back in his ears and nose. He flexed his toes and fingers to keep the blood flowing.

The cold wind was like a million tiny saws chewing into him. He ignored it, listened intently for the sound of a door latch.

After a half hour, a dull click, barely audible beneath the wind. He turned his head to peer through a gap between the logs. A light shone in the open back door. Two men came out, one stopping just beyond the door while the other—a broad-shouldered man in sleeve garters and an apron—moved toward the woodpile. Their shadows were long in the lamplit snow.

". . . and be fast about it," yelled the man by the door.

"Why don't you give me a hand?" said the man in the apron.

"How would I keep a gun on you?" The man by the door laughed.

The other man—a powerfully built man with a bull neck, walrus mustache, and a thatch of sandy, untrimmed hair—stepped between the two wings of the woodpile and grabbed a log off the top. He wore no hat or coat, and his striped shirtsleeves were rolled up his thick, tattooed arms. A bloody bandage covered his right ear. He knocked the snow off the log and was about to pick up another, when Hawk lifted his head above the pile.

The man jerked with a start, froze. Quickly, Hawk lifted a gloved finger to his lips. The man's heavy brows beetled.

"How many inside?" Hawk asked, raising his voice only loudly enough for the big man to hear.

"Who're you?"

"Answer the question."

"Twelve."

"All in one room?"

The barman slowly picked another log off the top of the pile. "There's two upstairs."

Hawk stole a quick glance around the barman. The man by the door was pissing, half-turned away from the wood pile, his rifle clamped under his right arm. Lamp-washed snow glittered on the shoulders of his rat-skin coat.

"Duck down," Hawk said.

"What?"

"Down!"

When the barman had crouched behind the short wing of the pile, Hawk leapt over the wood stacked before him, crouched down beside the barman, doffed his hat, and quickly removed his coat. "Stay here."

Tossing his coat over the barman's shoulders and laying his rifle in the snow, Hawk stood and, keeping

his back to the building, quickly gathered an armload
of wood. He started toward the hotel. The man by the
door was shaking himself, bouncing lightly on the
balls of his feet.

He glanced at Hawk, turned away, finished buttoning his fly. When Hawk was ten feet away from
him, he turned toward the open alley, taking his rifle
in both hands.

"I must be pissin' pure rye." He jerked his head at
the closed door. "Hurry it up—get in there!"

He stepped back to let Hawk go ahead of him,
then stopped suddenly, turned to Hawk sharply.
"Wha—?"

Hawk threw himself straight forward, lowering
his head, leaping off his heels, and bowling the man
over with his armload of wood. The man's back hit
the ground, Hawk on top of him, the split logs rolling
off the man's chest and face into the snow.

Hawk grabbed a log in his right hand, smashed it
savagely against the man's right jaw, opening up a
six-inch gash.

The man grunted and kicked. Bringing the log
back down from his left shoulder, Hawk smashed it
across the man's left temple, the bone cracking like a
gourd. After two more blows, the man's body relaxed
under Hawk's knees.

Nearby, snow crunched under boots. A rifle barrel
poked the back of Hawk's neck.

"Hold it right there," a familiar voice raked out.
"I'm a deputy United States marshal, and you're
under arrest."

15.

REUNION

IT took Hawk only a half second to place the voice. Morgan must not have recognized him, with the snow slashing down, clinging to Gideon's hair and clothes. But there was no doubt in Hawk's mind that the young marshal had followed him here.

"Raise your hand above your head," Morgan shouted above the wind.

Hawk raised his hands and was beginning to turn his head toward Morgan, when a shadow flicked behind the staircase, darted out from behind it. Light from the open door flashed off the rifle in the man's hands.

"Hold it!" the man shouted.

Hawk reached for his Russian, but before he could bring it up, the rifle flashed and cracked. Behind him, Morgan grunted and stumbled back in the snow. The gunman ran wide of the staircase landing and dropped to a knee as he levered a fresh shell in his carbine's breech. Hawk swung the Russian toward him, fired. The man flew back, throwing the rifle.

Hawk pushed to his feet and turned around. Morgan was down on one knee, head lowered, his left hand clutching his right shoulder. His rifle lay over one of the fallen logs.

Inside the hotel, boots pounded the floorboards. A rifle popped near the woodpile, the slug splintering wood from the frame of the back door, evoking a surprised yell from within as a head drew back and sideways.

The man in the apron, now wearing Hawk's coat and holding his rifle, beckoned broadly. "Hurry!"

Hawk started toward him, looked down at Morgan, who'd dropped to both knees. Cursing, Hawk crouched and threw the young marshal's left arm over his shoulder and straightened, Morgan grunting painfully.

Staggering under the cumbersome load, Hawk ran toward the big barman, who turned and ran a dozen yards beyond the woodpile before stopping to fire at the rear door of the hotel, the rifle cracking dully under the wind.

"Follow me," he yelled to Hawk, turning and running into the trees and brush beyond the privy.

Behind them, rifles popped almost inaudibly, the slugs plunking into the snowdrifted ground, one pinking a tin can in the trash mounded to Hawk's right. Soon they were tracing a circuitous route through widely spaced cabins, trees, and boulders, heading west, then north.

Hawk stopped several times to look behind. No one appeared to be following. Just as Hawk's back was about to give beneath Morgan's weight, a broad, gray barn took shape in the darkness.

The barman pushed a door open, then stepped aside as Hawk stumbled over the jamb, nearly falling. The barman came in, closed and barred the door, then led Hawk past several stalls and wagons and into a small, lamplit room at the back.

The kid Hawk had talked to earlier jumped up from a rolltop desk, clutching his chest. "Jesus Christ, Max, you nearly gave me a heart seizure!"

"Put him there," the barman told Hawk, pointing at a cot mounded with quilts, Army blankets, and a flat pillow.

Hawk eased Morgan onto the cot, which creaked beneath the deputy's weight, then slipped the law-man's Colts from his holster. With one hard jerk, he removed Morgan's right boot, reached into the well, and pulled the snub-nosed .36 from the sewn-in sheath. He tossed the boot aside, stuffed both weapons behind his cartridge belt.

"Goddamn fool," Hawk snarled. "Almost got yourself killed."

Clutching his bleeding shoulder, teeth gritted in pain, Morgan glared at him, not saying anything.

A poorly rolled cigarette smoldered in the ashtray atop the desk. The barman stubbed it out, lightly swatted the kid's head, hitting mostly hair. "What's your pa told you about smokin' in the barn?"

He turned to Hawk. "This is my nephew, Kenny. I'm Max Beardon, the weekday barman over to the Venus." He glanced at Morgan before returning his eyes to Hawk. "Who the hell are you two?"

"I'm U.S. Deputy Marshal Luke Morgan," Morgan said tightly, his eyes fixed on Hawk, "here on special assignment."

Hawk turned to Beardon. "I'm gonna need a bottle of whiskey, if you got any, and—"

Beardon grabbed Hawk's arm, cutting him off. The barman's face was flushed, his eyes pinched and miserable. "They forced me to tell them where Haskell lives."

Hawk glanced at the bloody bandage on Beardon's ear. It was soaked all the way through. "His family's fine for now," Hawk said. "Fetch that bottle and a basin with warm water, something I can use for bandages."

Beardon cut his befuddled gaze from Hawk to Morgan and back again, then doffed Hawk's hat, handed it to him. "You two have a mighty strange relationship." He turned, sent Kenny home to his parents, and began rummaging around the shelves to the right of the door.

Morgan was still staring up at Hawk, who tossed his hat onto a chair near the bullet-shaped stove at the back of the room. "What're you gonna do?" Morgan asked.

"If that bullet don't come out, you're gonna bleed to death."

"I'm here to *kill* you, Gideon."

Hawk chuffed. "Killing's against the law, Luke."

"I've got a paper, signed by four territorial governors."

"Well, then . . ."

Hawk turned as Beardon came up behind him with a corked whiskey bottle and a roll of bandages. Hawk took the bottle and the bandages, moved to the cot. He set the bandages on a small table cluttered with bits of harness and old magazines, propped one knee on the cot. Brusquely, he moved Morgan's right hand away from the wounded shoulder, opened his coat.

With a single jerk of his fist, he ripped the shirt and undershirt halfway down the young lawman's pale chest, peeled it back to reveal the bloody wound.

The bullet had gone in about four inches down from the top of the shoulder. Dark red blood welled up from the wound, dribbled down the lawman's chest. Morgan grimaced.

"This your first one, Luke?"

"Second. Don't you remember?"

"That's right. Curly Bill Turner nearly scraped a brow from your face with that old Spencer of his. Just couldn't stop sellin' whiskey on the rez. Well, that was nothin' compared to this."

"Bad?"

Hawk plucked the cork from the whiskey bottle

with his teeth, held the bottle out to Morgan. "Drink half o' that."

"I wanna stay sober."

"When I start pokin' around in that shoulder with my pig-sticker, you're gonna wanna be three sheets to the wind." Hawk held Morgan's pinched glare. "I dragged you all the way in here, when I should have left you out *there*, so drink up, kid."

"This won't stop me, Gid. I'm sorry about Linda and Jubal, but I'm here to kill you."

"You can kill me tomorrow."

Morgan's brown eyes, creased with revulsion, bored into Hawk's. "You're the worst kind of outlaw—the kind that tries to justify himself with a badge—and you have to be stopped."

Hawk shook the bottle, sloshing the whiskey around. "Shut up and drink before I let you bleed dry."

Morgan cursed, took the bottle, and tipped it back.

"Take another one."

Morgan took another drink. Hawk removed his stiletto from the sheath behind his neck, took the bottle, poured whiskey over the blade, then sloshed about a cup's worth over the wound. As the pain bit deep, Morgan's body stiffened, and he threw his head back and opened his mouth, exhaling a long, raspy groan.

Max Beardon had filled a washbasin with hot water from the stove, and set the basin and a soft, clean cloth on the table near Morgan's head. As Beardon, armed with Hawk's rifle, went outside to see if they'd been followed, Hawk soaked the cloth in the basin, cleaned most of the blood away from the wound, then slid the razor-sharp stiletto tip between the wound's ragged, bloody edges.

Morgan groaned, his sweat-soaked face bleaching as he scissored his legs and ground his fists into the cot. He took several more long pulls from the bottle. As Hawk slid the thumb and index finger of his left hand into the wound, the deputy continued to buck and kick.

Hawk plucked a .44 cartridge from Morgan's belt, slipped it between the deputy's mustachioed lips.

"Bite down."

Morgan bit down, nearly chewing through the brass casing as Hawk resumed probing the wound. Hawk fished around for several more minutes before the knife blade ticked the slug. Morgan grunted shrilly, and his body relaxed, eyelids closing, quivering for a few seconds before the deputy lost consciousness.

The cartridge fell from his lips.

Hawk pulled the knife from the wound, pressing the bloody slug to the blade with his left index finger. He dropped it in the basin with a plop.

"That's for old times, Luke." Hawk stuffed a clean bandage into the hole, pressed it down hard against the lawman's shoulder. "And it's the *last* time."

After Hawk finished dressing Morgan's wound, the young man slept while Gideon sat in a chair near the wood stove, sipping coffee he'd poured from the

small black percolator. He stared at the flames jumping and sparking behind the stove's dented door.

A door opened and closed in the main part of the
barn. Hawk's right hand closed over the grips of his
.44. When Beardon's jowly face appeared in the office doorway, Hawk removed his hand from the
Russian's grips.

Beardon wore a cloth watch cap and blanket coat
he'd stored in the barn—as he often worked week-
ends for his brother—and held an old Colt's revolv-
ing rifle in his gloved hands.

"Nothin' out there."

Hawk sipped his coffee. "By now, they know *I'll*
be coming for *them*."

"You're goin' back there?" Beardon's deep voice
was pitched with exasperation.

Hawk drained his coffee cup, stood, and reached
for his rifle.

Beardon stepped toward him. "I say we head south
of town, hole up in a cabin, and wait for Haskell. The
three of us against that gang is better odds than you
alone."

Hawk shook his head. "I'm gonna finish it tonight . . .
alone."

"See now, I savvied from your conversation with
him"—Beardon canted his head at Morgan—"who
you are. I never approved of what you do—huntin'
down killers and killin' 'em without a trial—but that
was before La Salle came here. Most folks around
didn't think Haskell shoulda hunted down Little Bob.
But I did. I stand by him. I'm goin' with you."

Again, Hawk shook his head. "If they come here and find Morgan, they're liable to burn the place. Stay put and keep that rifle handy." Hawk snugged his hat down tight, hefted his rifle, and turned to the door.

"Hold on. There's a way into the hotel La Salle don't know about. I was figurin' on usin' it later in the night, to get the girls out."

After a brief discussion, Hawk left Beardon sitting in the office chair, sipping coffee, the old Colt's rifle across his thighs. Gideon scurried through the blowing and drifting snow, retracing his and the barman's previous route, until he'd made his way back to the alley behind the hotel. He took a quick reconnaissance from the woodpile, then ran to the building's left rear corner.

He kicked away the snow and gravel from two cellar doors, grabbed the ring of one, and pulled. It wouldn't budge more than an inch. Setting his rifle aside, Hawk pulled with both hands, gritting his teeth and feeling the wound in his left arm open slightly, blood dribbling out from behind the bandage.

The unoiled hinges barked, the door gave suddenly, opening on a dark hole smelling of rotten potatoes, stale whiskey, and earth.

Hawk held the half-open door with one hand, and grabbed his rifle. After spotting a set of half-rotten wooden steps, he descended the hole, drawing the door closed behind him. Anyone strolling around the building would find the exposed doors, but it was a chance he'd have to take.

In the stygian darkness at the bottom of the steps, he hunkered down, removed a glove, and lit a match. The flickering light revealed low, wooden rafters, cobwebs, and a dusty stone floor spotted with rat shit and occasional shards from broken bottles.

He rose to a half crouch and moved forward, his rifle in his right hand, the match in the left. When the match burned out, he stopped, lit another, and continued forward until another short set of wooden steps took shape in the darkness. Directly above the steps was a plank door, four feet long by two feet wide.

Through the cracks he smelled cooked food, heard muffled voices. He dropped the match, set his rifle against the wall, and set the heels of both hands against the door.

As he started to slowly push, boots pounded the floorboards to his right, heading toward the cellar door. Hawk lowered his hands a few inches and peered up through a crack as the boots pounded across the door, loosing dust from between the cracks, then continued several feet farther on.

Almost directly above Hawk, the man said, "I say we go on out there—every last one of us—and scour the town for that son of a bitch."

Canting a strained glance through a door crack, Gideon could see only a boot and a spur, the frayed cuff of damp deerskin pants. From the clatter and scrape of pots and utensils, the man was preparing food.

A voice rose from the main room, but Hawk couldn't make out the words.

"I know, I know," the man above Hawk said as he slapped a lid down on an iron pot. "Let him come to us. . . ."

The man's boots pounded back the way they'd come.

Hawk squatted there on the cellar floor, listening. The muffled voices continued in the other room. No footsteps headed this way.

He set his hands against the door and gently pushed.

16

INTO THE LION'S DEN

HAWK pushed up hard with the heels of his hands.

The door wouldn't budge.

He lowered his head and lifted his shoulders, pressing his back against the door planks and pushing up from his knees. He puffed his cheeks out with the effort. Blood trickled from the wound down his right arm.

The door cracked and groaned, gave a scraping, belching sound as it popped free of its frame. Hawk froze, the weight of the door on his back, peering through the three-inch gap between the door and the frame.

Seeing no one in the room, he continued straightening his knees, then climbed the steps, until he'd opened the door a good four feet. He held it open with his rifle, slipped through the gap onto the main floor, then, hooking a gloved finger through the handle ring, eased it back down to its frame.

He straightened and looked around the small, rectangular room.

According to Beardon, it was the original saloon, when Skinners' Bottoms was only a hide-hunters' camp. It was old and shabby, with a grease-splattered iron range on which a big iron pot sat, steam rising from its lid, smelling like burned stew. There were a couple of narrow wooden tables, whiskey casks, shelves swollen with bottles and canned goods. Pots and pans hung from rusty nails. Initials and dates as far back as the '40s had been carved into the log walls.

Voices drifted through the door curtain to the main room. There were the sounds of men eating, belching, and playing cards.

Someone slapped pasteboards onto a table with a sharp crack. "If that bastard keeps whittling us down, we ain't gonna ride out of here with but four or five men!"

"And a woman!" added a husky female voice.

"That's why we're sittin' tight," said another man, smacking his lips after drinking. "Let him come to us."

"What if he don't come to us?"

"Then, tomorrow, when it gets light and this storm has died down, we'll go lookin' fer *him*! Relax, Comanche. I see it all plain now, an' I ain't in such a hurry. Have another cup o' joe."

As Hawk cat-footed to the far side of the kitchen,

the man called Comanche said he didn't want any more coffee, he wanted a drink. Hawk stepped into a small, dark pantry and looked up.

The old chimney hole, which Beardon had told him about, was a black circle, about two feet in diameter, in the pantry's ceiling, above the shelves of dry goods and crates and two oak flour bins.

"No more drinkin'," ordered La Salle. "I want everybody sober for the rest of the night."

"What about ruttin'?" asked the husky-voiced woman sarcastically—no doubt Ed's half sister, Babe.

"Ruttin's all right," Ed said. "Sobers the boys up—keeps 'em alert . . . as long as they ain't all upstairs at once."

Hawk drew the pantry's curtain closed, set his rifle against the wall, started pulling one of the flour bins into the middle of the niche, and stopped. Footsteps approached from the main room. He turned to the curtain.

It had been open when he got here. Should he open it again now, and hide?

Too late.

Babe Mayberry's voice rose as she approached the kitchen. "I don't think all this fuckin's fair when we all can't participate. I done fucked every one of these fellers, and you know how I hate fuckin' the same feller twice!"

Her guffaws were loud as cannon blasts as she entered the kitchen, her squat shape visible through the thin, flour-sack curtain. Swinging her stubby arms, she strode across the room. The pot's lid clanked on the range.

Slopping stew into her tin bowl, Babe muttered, "And I ain't in the mood for no more *female* companionship. . . ."

Hawk stood behind the curtain, squeezing his rifle, holding his breath, and hoping his outline was concealed by the shadows behind him. When Babe had returned the lid to the pot, she turned her head toward the pantry. Hawk couldn't see her eyes, but he could tell she was staring toward him.

Hawk's heart thudded. She was wondering why the curtain was closed.

Very observant bitch . . .

Slowly, she started moving toward the pantry. Hawk set his thumb on the Henry's hammer. He started to draw it back.

La Salle yelled from the next room, "Come on, Babe—it's your deal!"

Six feet from the curtain, Babe stopped, then wheeled away and stalked out of the kitchen.

"I'm comin'," she grouched. "Can't a girl get a bite to eat around here?"

Hawk removed his thumb from the hammer, took a breath, and leaned his rifle against the wall. He removed his hat and coat, dropped both to the floor, then stooped and pulled the flour bin out from the wall, inching it along to keep the noise down.

When he had it beneath the chimney hole, he grabbed his rifle, hoisted himself up, wincing against the pain in his right arm, and peered up at the hole only six inches beyond his nose.

Beardon had told him the hole opened into the corner of one of the girls' rooms in the second story. It was covered with a braided rug. Poking at the hole, Hawk found that there wasn't anything else over the hole, just the rug.

He could tell from the moans, grunts, and bed squawks that one of the girls was entertaining. They sounded far enough away from the hole, however, that if the room was dark, he should be able to get through the hole and the rug without being seen.

Using his rifle, he poked the rug away from the opening. He pushed the rifle up through the hole, slid it quietly along the floor, then stuck his head through the hole into the room.

Luck smiled at him.

The hole was only a foot from the outside wall. Between the hole and the two couplers on the bed was a small table draped with white lace and topped with a tintype and a single candle that cast most of the room in shadow.

The bed was shoved into the room's far corner. If the man turned his head and looked closely, he'd probably see Hawk, but that was an outside chance. The man, whose eyes were squeezed shut, seemed to be thoroughly enjoying himself between the girl's dimpled knees.

"You favored that deputy, did you, girl?" he said tightly. The dove whimpered, the springs singing beneath her. "No damn badge-toter can give it to you like I can. . . ."

"Can't you just hurry it *up*?" the girl pleaded.

Hawk was hoisting himself up from the hole, using both hands and moving slowly.

"No, I can't just hurry it up," the man mocked. "You know how long I been forkin' a saddle? Wouldn't hurt if you'd put a little enthusiasm into it."

"I done told ya I wasn't interested."

As Hawk lifted a leg out of the hole, the man bucked savagely into the girl. With one hand, he jerked her head back with a fistful of hair. "Maybe I'll take you with me when we leave here . . . how'd that . . . be . . . ?"

Hawk crouched in the shadows beside the table. His voice was level and quiet. "The girl don't seem to be in the mood tonight, champ."

"Huh?"

The man jerked his head toward Hawk, who reached behind his neck, unsheathed the stiletto, and flung it toward the bed. The blade glinted copper in the lamplight as it tumbled end over end toward the bed and buried itself hilt-deep in the man's throat, pinning his neck to the wall on the far side of the bed.

The man's eyes snapped wide. He wasn't much over twenty—patch-bearded, mean-eyed. Choking sounds rose from his throat. His bare legs kicked on the bed, his balbriggans knotted around his ankles. His red tool wilted like a wildflower in a snowstorm.

He lifted his right hand to the stiletto blade, as if to remove it. The hand stopped as it touched the blade, then dropped slowly to the bed, where it rested, palm up.

Hawk straightened, glanced at the girl.

She'd scuttled back against the headboard and curled into a ball, shuttling her horrified gaze between Hawk and his quarry. Hawk pressed a finger to his lips, but then he saw that she was too scared to scream. Picking up his rifle, he strode to the bed, looked down at the gang member, who stared up at him helplessly. Blood gushed down his neck and between the two hairy slabs of his chest.

He moved his lips as if to speak, but no words came out.

When Hawk extended his right hand toward him, the man's right foot twitched. Hawk closed his hand over the stiletto's handle, pressed the butt of his rifle against the man's forehead, and pulled the blade from the wall and the man's throat with a jerk.

The man slid sideways down to the bed, leaving a bloody smear on the wall above.

Hawk cleaned the stiletto on the man's balbriggans.

"Who are you?" she asked quietly, resting her head on her arms. Her legs were curled so tightly that her knees nearly touched her chin.

"A friend."

"Lawman?"

"That's right."

Hawk returned the knife to its sheath, grabbed one of the dead man's ankles, and pulled his body onto

the floor. He lifted the sheets and quilts over the cow-
ering girl's small, pale body.

"They killed Stokeley and Cushman." With the
thumb and index finger of her left hand, the girl
flicked lint from the sheets. Then she licked her lips.
"Shot 'em, stuffed their bodies down the privy." Her
lips quivered, and tears came to her eyes. "They
come in laughing about it."

Holding his rifle in both hands, Hawk stared down
at her. "Where are the other girls?"

"Locked in their rooms—most of 'em. That
woman killed Camille. Shot her in the street, left her
there."

Hawk turned to the door, opened it a crack, and
peered both ways down the hall lit by two shimmer-
ing lanterns. There was a red runner smelling like
spilled beer and cigarette smoke. Hawk stepped out,
pulled the door closed behind him.

To his left rose the clack of boots on the stone
steps, and a shadow grew on the wall across from the
stairs. Quickly, Hawk turned, opened the door of
the room he'd just left, and stepped inside. He kept
the door cracked, peered with one eye into the hall.

A man appeared at the top of the stairs, striding
swiftly toward Hawk, a cigarette dangling from his
teeth. He wore a flat-brimmed hat and red and green
poncho. "Come on, Bryce, goddamnit. You've taken
long enough." He stopped at a nearby room, pounded
the door once, and went in. "Come on, Bryce—"

A pistol shot cut him off. He bolted back into the
hall and drew the door closed behind him. His ciga-

rette was gone and his hat was askew. There was a
small, round hole through the door's top panel.

He smacked the door with his fist and continued
down the hall toward Hawk. "Owly son of a *bitch*!"

Hawk watched the man stride toward him, the
man's face bunched with anger. "Come on, Alvis!
Let me have a time, goddamnit!"

When he was six feet from the door, Hawk
stepped behind it, pressed his back to the wall. Beside him, a belted pink robe hung from a hook.
Quickly, he slipped the belt from the robe, stretched
it taut between his hands.

The door bolted open. The man came through,
heading for the bed. "Ed ain't lettin' us come up but
two at a time, and Bryce won't . . . !"

He stopped, stared down at the man on the floor.
As he reached for the pearl-gripped .45 on his hip,
Hawk rushed up behind him, swung the belt over his
head, jerked it tight around his neck, and sawed back
on both ends.

The man grabbed at Hawk's hands as he stumbled
backward, losing his hat and his footing, hitting the
floor on his butt.

Hawk dropped to one knee, crossed the belt ends
behind the man's head, and jerked them taut. The
man kicked and thrashed as he choked. His windpipe
shut, he wound down like a clock. The muscles
slowly relaxed. His hands opened, slid from Hawk's
wrists, and dropped to the puncheons. Under the
striped poncho, his shoulders sagged.

Hawk's grip on the belt remained firm. The man's

head lolled against Gideon's knee, and his face in the guttering lamplight turned blue behind his beard. His tongue drooped toward the floor.

Hawk let the man's head sag to the floor. He released the belt, slipped the poncho over the man's shoulders, and dropped it over his own. He liked the fit if not the smell. If he didn't get back to his coat, however, he was going to need something warm.

Hawk retrieved his rifle from the wall behind the door, glanced at the girl. She was in the same position she'd been in when he'd left the room the first time.

He turned and went out.

17

VENUS FANDANGO

HAWK paused at the door with the hole in it. Hearing only rustling clothes inside the room, he continued down the hall and stopped at the top of the stairs. Beyond the landing was a balcony over the saloon's main hall. From below rose voices and the sounds of cardplaying and the blue webs of tobacco and wood smoke.

He padded across the landing, pressed his back against a stone pillar on the far side of the stairs, and slid a glance over the wrought-iron rail and into the main hall, getting a rough understanding of the layout, including the men's positions, in two quick seconds.

Hawk turned, walked back down the hall, stopped at the same door he'd stopped at before, and slowly turned the knob.

When the bolt clicked, he swung the door wide, raked a quick glance around the dusky, candlelit room fetid with sex, whiskey, cigar smoke, and sweet perfume. The man sat at the foot of the bed, pulling a wool sweater over his head, facing the wall to Hawk's right. The girl was standing naked before a dresser, taking a sponge bath, her back to the door.

Hawk strode toward the man, taking his Henry's barrel in both hands. As the man turned toward the sound of Hawk's footsteps, his head popped out of the top of the sweater—a wide, white scar cutting through his cherry-red beard.

"She's all yours, Chick, you impatient son of a—"

Hawk swung the rifle butt from right to left, connecting soundly with the bearded man's head. The man yelped as blood sprayed from his split skull. He tumbled across the bed, hitting the floor on the other side with a slap and a dull thud.

Wheeling toward Hawk, the girl gave a clipped "*Oh!*" and, dropping her sponge, grabbed the edge of the dresser behind her. She did nothing to cover herself, just stared at Hawk with a mix of fear and befuddlement, her mussed hair in her eyes.

Hawk flipped his rifle around, ran out the open door and down the hall. Downstairs, a man's voice boomed, "What the hell is goin' on up there? Cain, get down here!"

Babe Mayberry laughed. "Don't you boys know how to behave in civilized society?"

Hawk pressed his back to the pillar, holding the Henry across his chest.

"Chick!" La Salle shouted. "This is no time for foolishness!"

Hawk turned to his left, facing the wrought-iron rail, staring into the main hall below. Everyone in the room, except the five men hog-tied on the floor, saw him at the same time, their hat brims rising as their chins came up.

Levering a round, Hawk raised the Henry to his shoulder, planted the front site square on Ed La Salle's chest, adjusted the back site till the front sight fitted snugly into the V, and squeezed the trigger.

La Salle's eyebrows rose and his lower jaw dropped at the same time the rifle leapt in Gideon's hands, the explosion rocking the room.

La Salle held a lit stogie in one hand, fanned pasteboards in the other. The stogie flew one way, the cards the other, as Hawk's bullet blew La Salle straight back in his chair. The outlaw leader turned a backward somersault and hit the floor on his chest, his bald head facing the table, his long body lying still as fresh cow plop.

Silence.

Babe and the men turned to La Salle, shock etched on their faces.

Babe opened her mouth, the cigar in her lips dropping to the table, where it rolled around the empty beer mugs and coffee cups. *"Ed!"*

The exclamation was a call to battle, jolting the other ten or so gang members out of their stupors. In the periphery of his vision, Hawk saw them bolt out of their chairs and claw iron as he levered a fresh shell into the Henry's breech and drew a bead on Babe.

As he took up the slack in his trigger finger, Babe bolted toward her dead brother. Another gang member—a skinny gent with close-cropped blond hair and one bloody arm in a sling—stepped between her and Hawk as he reached for a rifle. Hawk's slug drilled him through one ear, blood and brain spraying out the other as he tumbled over the table, as loose-limbed as a corn-shuck doll.

As the man and the table went down in a shower of cups, mugs, cards, and ashtrays, Hawk brought his Henry's barrel back behind the railing, and ducked.

Pistols and rifles exploded below, drowning out the shouted curses and orders. The slugs plunked into the timbered ceiling above Hawk, and into the adobe wall behind him. Several sparked off the rail, ringing shrilly and peppering his face with lead and iron shards.

Hawk crawled back behind the balcony's lip. He crawled to his right, staying low enough that the bullets hammering up from below careened over his head and into the wall and doors and into the dusty Mexican tapestries hanging behind him.

When most of the slugs were arcing over the balcony near the stairs, he levered a fresh shell, rose to one knee, and aimed through the powder smoke wafting up from below. He picked out a target hun-

kered down behind a blood-splattered chair, and
fired.

The slug clipped through the chair with an angry
pop. The man behind it tensed, dropped his two pistols, and grabbed his throat with both hands.

Hawk turned his head slightly right as a pistol
stabbed smoke and flames at him. The man wielding
the silver-plated Smith & Wesson was half hidden by
an adobe support post bedecked with chili peppers
and Chinese lanterns.

Flinching at the nip in his left side, Hawk
squeezed off a shot toward the support post. His slug
sparked off the Smithy's cylinder. The man stumbled
out from behind the post, wincing and grabbing his
right wrist. Gideon shot him just above his left ear,
then hammered the room with seven more shots before the Henry's hammer clicked, empty.

Without hesitation, Hawk whipped the rifle into
the room below, leapt onto the wrought-iron railing,
then jumped straight out over the floor and caught a
chandelier cable in both gloved hands. Entwining his
feet around the cable, he dropped straight down the
line to within a half foot of the flickering glass
globes.

He stopped, threw his body forward, and releasing
the cable, kicked off one of the copper gas canisters.
As the chandelier swayed wildly above him, flinging
shadows and kerosene about the room, Hawk hit the
floor on his feet. Diving forward to avoid the lead
buzzing around his ears, he bulled a gunman into an

overturned table, rolled off a shoulder, and came up filling his hands with pistols from both holsters.

With his Russian, he shot the man he'd knocked flat. With the Colt, he checked the charge of a broad, lumbering Indian leaping toward him with a big bowie in his teeth. Hawk dropped to a knee and, triggering both guns in turn, shot at the gun flashes and jostling shadows inside the growing smoke cloud, the smell of cordite nearly pinching off his wind.

Around him, men shouted and screamed. Babe Mayberry was yelling like a poleaxed heifer from somewhere to Hawk's right. He triggered a couple of shots in her direction, but because of all the smoke and debris, he couldn't tell if he'd hit his mark.

When his pistols were nearly empty, he bolted off his right knee and ran, pivoting and firing, toward the front window. He turned, fired one more shot with both pistols, then lowered his head and dove through the shade-covered window, the screech of breaking glass rising around him, shards cutting into his face and arms.

He hit the snowy stoop on his right shoulder, rolled, gained his feet, shook his head to clear the cobwebs, then ran right of the window and into the darkness beyond the hotel.

A man shouted behind him, loosed a shot.

Hawk turned left behind a wagon loaded with firewood, and sprinted across the street, twice nearly slipping in the snow or tripping over buried rocks.

At the corner of a building, he stopped, peered back toward the saloon. A man was stepping through the broken window, a pistol reflecting the lamplight from inside.

"He went that way!" he yelled, his voice ripped by the wind, his hat blowing off.

Leaving the hat, he began moving in Hawk's direction, following Hawk's fresh tracks and peering warily along both sides of the street.

Hawk pulled back behind the building, pressed his back to the whipsawed boards, and began reloading the Russian. He thumbed the shells from his cartridge belt and through the pistol's open loading gate, the process quickly growing awkward as the cold, knifing wind numbed his fingers.

He had the Russian loaded and was working on the Colt Army when he heard the man's boots crunch snow. He plucked two more shells from his belt, punched the first one through the loading gate.

A shadow moved on his right, coming along the corner of the building.

Hunkering in the darkness at the building's base, Hawk punched the second shell home. Voices rose on the wind. One belonged to Babe Mayberry.

"Find him!" the woman screamed with rage. "I want him *found*!"

Hawk stood and ran straight back along the building, turned left as if to move behind it, then swung right. He stopped at the rear of a little adobe cabin, peered around the corner and into the space he'd just traversed. The man following him was an indiscernible shape in the blowing snow and darkness.

When he came to the rear of the building across

the space from Hawk, he turned to swing wide of the corner.

"Ready to die?" Hawk shouted.

The man swung toward him. When he'd given his chest to Hawk, Gideon drilled his checked shirt with two well-placed rounds from each revolver. The man's own pistol popped a slug into the ground as he wheeled, screaming. Firing another round into the snow, he fell on his side and lay still.

In the corner of his right eye, Hawk saw several figures running past the gap between the buildings, heading east down the main street, away from the saloon. The swirling wind had told them the gun reports had come from farther north.

Hawk turned to follow. Beneath him, the snowy ground pitched. A wave of nausea washed over him. He stopped, pressed his back against the wall. He touched the wound, the cold blood chilling him, and winced.

He needed rest before he could finish the fight, but he didn't have the strength or enough warm clothes to make it back to the Haskell place.

Dragging his boot toes, he shuffled westward through the drifting snow, squinting against the wind that sucked each breath from his lungs. The gusts staggered him like a boxer's blows. Twice he stumbled and dropped to his knees.

He didn't know how much time had passed before he clawed his way inside the jailhouse's rear door. Fumbling with the knob, he drew the door closed behind him, and lowered the locking bar. Unable to feel his toes, he moved passed the cells to the dark front office.

He tripped over one of the dead men on the floor, dropped to his knees with a grunt. Biting his lip and holding his bloody left side, he regained his feet, then closed and locked the front door.

He paused for a moment, staring out the window, trying to formulate a plan. The cold and pain had slowed his thoughts.

He dropped a knee to the snow that had blown inside, and removed the dead deputy's neckerchief. Heaving himself up again with a pained wince, he staggered back to the cot that sat along the front wall.

He sat heavily down, lifted the poncho, pulled his shirttails out of his pants, and shoved an end of the neckerchief into the bloody hole in his side. He stemmed the blood but not the pain.

The wind shook the walls and windows, thumped the door in its frame. The stove chimney moaned and rattled.

Hawk slumped down on the cot, resting his head on the pillow. He lifted his legs, crossed his ankles, and filled his hands with both pistols.

He crossed the pistols on his belly, thumbs on the hammers, and closed his eyes. He listened for a time, hearing only the wind and the snow spraying the walls. The remaining gang members were scouring the town for him. Would they track him here?

He didn't care.

Fatigue washed over him.

In less than a minute, he slept.

18

DEADLY PREY

IN a dream, Hawk's wife, Linda, came to the little, storm-wracked jailhouse in Skinners' Bottoms, and cleaned and bandaged Gideon's wound. As always, she worked a long time, swabbing and stitching with the utmost, soothing care.

Like she'd done so many times before, she'd kissed the bandaged wound, then his forehead. She'd given him a cupful of whiskey, sat with him while he drank it, told him how she worried about him, then added another log to the stove. She kissed him again, squeezed his hands, drew the covers up tight beneath his chin, and went away to let him sleep. . . .

Outside, Hawk heard Jubal playing with his dog, and vaguely wondered why the boy would be outside on such a snowy night. But then, the boy had always loved the snow, as he'd loved his fishing hole and his horse carvings, and he'd never wandered far from the house. . . .

Horse hooves thudded softly.

Hawk opened his eyes, stared up at a low ceiling, squinting against bright sunlight angling through the sashed window in the wall to his left. As he blinked and felt the six-shooters in his hands, he remembered where he was and how he'd gotten there, all that had transpired last night in the Venus. The hoof falls were not rising from the street before his little house in Crossroads, but from the street before the jailhouse in Skinners' Bottoms. In a moment, all remnants of the dream faded, and he realized with a falling sensation that his dead family had not returned to him.

His wounded side was sticky, felt as though a knife were sticking out of it.

Outside, the hooves thudded louder.

He rose up on the cot and turned his head toward the bright, golden light twinkling like spangles on the snow covering the street before the jailhouse, and mounded like rich swirls of white icing on pediments and porch roofs, on the crates and rain barrels lining the unroofed boardwalks. It lay several inches thick on stock troughs and hitching posts.

A couple of feet had fallen, maybe more. Not a cloud remained, however, and already the sun was melting the snow above the window, dripping sparkling droplets onto the pane.

The pounding hooves approached from the right, with the soft spraying sound of flying snow. Hawk turned to see a rider approach, his star-faced black lumbering through the heavy drifts.

Horse and rider continued on past the jailhouse and pulled up before the Venus. The rider shucked a glove from his hand, stuck two fingers into his mouth, and whistled. He sat, waiting, staring at the hotel's front door, then anxiously waved his hand in the direction from which he'd come.

The hotel's front door opened and Babe Mayberry stepped out—short and squat, holding a Winchester carbine in her gloved hands.

"Not a half a mile away," the rider said, his voice clear in the snowy morning silence. "Comin' on fast, like he's anxious to get home."

"You git on over to the jailhouse," Babe ordered, nodding her head in Hawk's direction. "He'll probably head thataway first."

"I reckon."

"And wipe that sour look off your face, goddamn you! We came here to do a job, and we're gonna do it! Now you get over there and let me see some *spring* in your *step*!"

The rider dismounted, shaking his head, moving as though he were running through deep water.

Babe spit a tobacco quid on the porch floor, peered cautiously up and down the street, then ran her gaze up along the roofline above the other board-walk before turning awkwardly and limping back inside the hotel.

The rider brushed snow from the tie rail before the saloon, then looped his reins over it. Shucking a

Sharps carbine from his saddle boot, he began trudging through the drifts, angling toward the jailhouse, the powdery snow winging up around his high, black boots.

Hawk holstered his revolvers, pressed the neckerchief deeper into his wounded side, and moved to the door. Quietly, he removed the locking bar, set it against the wall, then slid the Russian from the cross-draw holster on his left hip, and stepped behind the door.

Outside, the man stomped the boardwalk to remove the snow from his boots. He turned the knob, shoved the door open, and stepped inside, closing the door with one hand as he moved to the window. He stopped suddenly, dropped his gaze to the cot beneath the window. Hawk's blood stained the rumpled Army blanket.

As the man began to turn his head to look behind, Hawk raised the Russian over his head, brought it down barrel-first against the man's snuff-brown hat. It was a hard, glancing blow.

The man yowled and dropped to a knee. Hawk hit him again. The carbine clattered to the split-pine floor as his quarry dropped to both hands and knees.

"Oh," he mumbled, squeezing his eyes closed. His hat had fallen off and his head sagged down between his shoulders. His long, tangled hair swept the floorboards.

"You wanna be addled for the rest of your life?" Hawk asked him, crouching over the man's left shoulder.

"What do you want?"

"How many of your gang are left?"

Face taut with pain, eyes slitted, the man looked up at him. "Go to hell!"

Hawk hit him again, with more of the Russian than before. The man dropped to his chest with a grunt. Blood shone in his hair, dripping under the coyote-fur collar of his coat.

"One more of those," Hawk said, "and you'll be wearing a bib to catch your drool." He grabbed a fistful of the man's thin hair and pulled his head back savagely. He lowered his face to the man's left ear. "How many are left?"

"Three."

"You sure?"

The man swallowed, winced against the pain, nodded.

"Good enough."

Hawk raised the Russian and slammed it butt-first against the crown of the man's head. His muscles were still jumping when Hawk stood and retrieved the Sharps carbine from the floor. Making sure a heavy-caliber bullet was snugged inside the chamber, he knelt on the cot and peered through the moisture-streaked window.

On the other side of the street, a tall man in a buffalo coat and flat-brimmed leather hat was walking westward along the boardwalk before a drugstore and a harness shop. Carrying a Winchester high across his chest, he stopped directly across from the jailhouse. He set the rifle down, pulled a rain barrel away from a wooden rain spout angling down from the boardwalk, and positioned it just right of the drugstore's three steps, mounded with glistening snow.

He looked west, adjusted the barrel's position slightly, then brushed snow off the drugstore's top step and sat down. He held the rifle across his knees, the barrel and the store's facade shielding him from the west.

Movement drew Hawk's eye farther west, and up to the skyline, where another man—stocky and wearing a long-sleeved wool shirt and long deer-skin vest—moved along the roof of McGillacartie's Tonsorial Parlor and Dental Practice, a squat yellow building of whipsawed boards nearly buried in snow.

The man dropped to his knees on the flat roof, looked around, adjusted his shabby bowler, scratched his beard, and lay down on his belly. From this van-tage, Hawk could see only his hat and the top of his forehead, around which a white bandage had been wrapped. The chimney and the roof line no doubt concealed him from the west.

Hawk looked at the saloon.

The front doors were closed. The sun reflected off the dark glass of the door and the big, main win-dow on which the gold-leaf lettering shone brightly. The black horse stood before the hitch rack, turned slightly toward Hawk and pawing at the snow as if to turn up grass.

Hawk leaned left and turned his head right, to peer westward along Main, seeing only snow. He tapped the single-shot Sharps in his hands. If he only had the sixteen-shot Henry . . .

He turned his gaze to the far wall, where three Winchesters and an old, trapdoor Springfield stood in a chained rack. A padlock secured them; breaking the padlock would require a shot. Out of the question.

In the distance, a horse blew. Hawk turned again toward the street, where the black whinnied and peered west, swishing its tail and pricking its ears.

In the drugstore's recessed entrance, the man in the buffalo coat leaned far back and ran his left hand up and down his rifle's forestock. The man on the roof of the tonsorial parlor had turned himself slightly west, as he hunkered down even lower than before. Hawk could see the tip of his rifle barrel.

Hawk canted a gaze west along Main, saw the horseback figure in the red mackinaw and bullet-crowned hat heading toward the jailhouse. Hawk's heart thudded as he glanced from the man atop the tonsorial parlor to the one on the drugstore step.

Which one should he try for first?

He ran to the door, pulled it open, and dropped to a knee. *"Haskell—it's an ambush!"*

As Hawk raised the Sharps to his shoulder, the hole in his side stitching painfully, a rifle cracked the morning quiet, echoing shrilly around the storefronts.

Pigeons flew up from the hotel's roof.

A horse screamed.

Hawk planted his sights on the man behind the barrel. As the man swung toward him, bringing his rifle around, Hawk fired.

The heavy round smashed the man's right shoulder with a solid *whunk!* laying him flat against the step, screaming. Several pistol shots rose on Hawk's right. Gideon swung his gaze that way.

The man in the mackinaw sat on the ground, one leg curled beneath the other, his horse fleeing behind him, reins trailing. The man aimed two pistols at the roof of the tonsorial parlor. The right one was smoking. Haskell extended the Colt in his left hand, thumbing back the hammer, and fired. The shot echoed flatly.

Hawk turned to the man on the drugstore step. The man's shoulder was bloody. Breathing like a landed fish, he heaved himself up and extended his right hand toward his rifle, half-buried in the snow of the boardwalk. Hawk moved toward him, striding swiftly in spite of the thudding heart in his side, and extended both pistols.

As the man, grunting and wheezing, brought up his rifle, Hawk closed on him and extended both pistols straight out from his chest. He fired the Russian, then the Colt, the slugs punching through the man's bear coat and laying him out for keeps.

The Venus's door rattled at the same time the man atop the tonsorial parlor screamed. In the corner of his right eye, Hawk saw a body fall, heard the soft thud in the snowy street. He turned left, extending the Russian toward the Venus.

Babe stepped out from the recessed doorway, turned toward him, raising her carbine, her eyes on fire.

"Bushwhackin' son of a *bitch*!"

The rifle cracked, the slug plunking into the corner of the drugstore behind Hawk's right shoulder. Hawk squeezed the Russian's trigger. The slug skidded off the barrel of Babe's rifle, screeching and sparking. Screaming, Babe dropped the rifle and stumbled back against the front wall, throwing her bare hands to her face. They came away bloody as she looked at Hawk, brown eyes big as mule shoes.

Hawk moved toward her, his strides slow and steady, both pistols at his sides.

Shaking and squealing, Babe turned, fumbled with the door.

Hawk raised the Colt and squeezed off a shot. It drilled the side of the door as Babe opened it and stumbled inside the saloon.

Gideon heard Babe's boots clacking the stone floor within. He grabbed the right door, swung it open, stepped inside, saw Babe's bulky figure retreating into the shadows toward the back of the cluttered, blood-washed room in which the bodies still lay from the night before.

She grunted and sighed, her voice quivering. Tripping over a man's leg, she fell to her knees and elbows, sobbing. A pistol lay to her right. She grabbed it and, still on her knees and propped on her right hand, aimed at Hawk and fired, the slug shattering what was left of the glass in the doors behind him.

Hawk fired the Colt, the slug sailing wide as Babe ducked, screaming and extending her own pistol. She pulled the trigger. The hammer clacked tinnily against the firing pin.

She pushed her thick body to her feet, whipped the pistol at Hawk, turned, and ran deeper into the shadows at the back of the saloon. Hawk moved down the bar, stepping over bodies and around broken tables and chairs. When Babe was at the bar's other end, he fired the Colt.

Babe screamed and fell, pressing her right hand to the back of her neck.

Hawk approached her.

She lay on her belly, kicking her legs and thrashing her arms, as if trying to dog-paddle across a raging stream. She turned her bloody face to him, stared, her mouth opening and closing but no words coming out.

She cleared her throat, licked her lips, one mouth corner lifting with a wan smile. "Y-you wouldn't kill a girl, would you, mister?"

Hawk pulled the Russian's trigger. A neat round hole appeared in Babe's right temple.

Her head whipped flat against the floor, wide-open eyes staring at the stones beneath her. She coughed, gurgled, twitched a few times, and lay still, her eyes remaining open, glaring.

"LIKE THE KILL-CRAZY

WOLF YOU ARE!"

HAWK turned away from Babe Mayberry, took a long look around the room. The five men, hog-tied along the far wall, regarded him warily, looking haggard and bleach-faced.

"Mister," one of them rasped, "think you c-could find it in your heart . . . to free us?"

Hawk holstered his pistol, cut the ropes binding the men, each crying out horrifically as the blood surged back into their starved limbs, then retrieved his coat and hat from the kitchen pantry, then found his Henry rifle on the floor beneath the balcony, leaning across the knee of one of the dead gang members. Walking along the bar to the front of the room, he turned to the blanket-covered body sprawled on the bar top.

He stopped, peeled the blanket back from the blue-white face. Ed La Salle's chest was matted with thick, jellied blood. The half-open eyes stared ruefully into Hawk's.

Hawk shrugged into his coat, donned his hat, and moved to the door. Broken glass crunching beneath his boots, he pulled the right door open, stepped outside. Wick Haskell was angling toward him from the left, the sniper from the roof of the tonsorial parlor lying bloody in the street behind him.

Hawk sensed more than saw movement on his right—a man moving along the broken-out front window, a rifle in his hands.

"Look out!" Haskell shouted. He stopped and crouched, swinging a revolver up.

Hawk turned his head right. Morgan stood frozen, a savage grimace lifting his red mustache as he stared down the barrel of an old Spencer rifle at Hawk. The look on the young deputy's face was so cold and heartless, that for a moment Hawk thought he must be one of the La Salle gang.

Gideon's heart leapt. He turned to Haskell, who'd stopped near the hitch rack, extending a long-barreled Colt in his right hand.

"No!" Hawk shouted.

Haskell's Colt barked a quarter second later, a sixteenth of a second before Morgan's rifle cracked, singeing nap from the crown of Gideon's hat. The sheriff's Colt spoke again, placing a second shot through Morgan's fawn vest, just beneath his deputy marshal's badge. The first shot had pierced his neck, from which blood gushed like a geyser.

"No!" Hawk shouted again, frozen, both hands up, his heart turning somersaults as he watched the young deputy slowly wheel, knees buckling as he backed up to an awning support post. He slid to the snowy boardwalk, stared up at Gideon, wide-eyed, then slumped over on his shoulder.

Blood turned the snow beneath him to a reddish-brown slush.

"He was about to shoot you," Haskell said, stepping up onto the boardwalk, his boots and trouser cuffs caked with snow.

A big man with a slight paunch and a thin, red-blond beard, he was breathing hard. He brushed past Hawk, glancing at him with puzzled eyes, then knelt down beside Morgan, whose chest had stopped rising and falling. He turned his head slowly to stare up at Hawk, his eyes now horrified as well as befuddled.

Haskell's voice was pinched with exasperation. "This man's a deputy U.S. marshal."

His heart thudding dully, Hawk stared down at Morgan, slumped and dead.

A woman's voice rose across the street. "Wick!"

Hawk turned to see Jesse Haskell riding toward the saloon on her raw-boned dun, her breath puffing in the sunshine. As the woman approached, Hawk moved off down the boardwalk, stepping around Morgan, then leaving the boardwalk and angling across the street, toward the livery barn. He stopped when he saw Max Beardon moving toward him around an empty hog pen, rubbing the back of his neck.

"The young marshal . . . knocked me out . . . took the rifle," the big man groused, wincing. "Did you see him?"

Hawk brushed past him, swaying a little from the wound in his side, the blood dripping down his right leg, and continued on to the livery barn.

He paid the boy, Kenny, an extra dime to saddle his horse. He didn't bother with the pack animal. Ten minutes later, he walked the grulla through the knee-high drifts, slumped forward in his saddle, holding the wound closed with his left hand.

Haskell and Jesse sat side by side on the porch steps of the Venus. Morgan lay on the porch to their left.

Jesse lifted her gaze toward Hawk. She started to get up, but stopped when Haskell grabbed her arm. The sheriff stood and, his broad, bearded face pinched with anger, stomped through the snow toward Hawk.

"Jesse told me who you are," Haskell said, glaring up at him.

Hawk turned to the man slowly, but said nothing.

Haskell glanced at Morgan, then returned his enraged eyes to Hawk. "I killed that lawman to save you. A vigilante. A rogue. *Damn* your hide!"

Jesse stood. "Wick, no . . ."

Hawk turned to stare over his horse's head. Haskell reached up and grabbed his saddle horn.

He shoved his face up toward Hawk's. "You ride on, you son of a bitch. If I ever catch you in my county again, I'm gonna take you in or gun you down like the kill-crazy wolf you are."

"Wick . . ." Jesse said.

Haskell released Hawk's saddle horn. "Get the hell out of my county!"

Hawk sat frozen for a time, staring over the grulla's twitching ears, pushing on the wound with the heel of his hand. He touched his spurs to the horse's sides, and the mustang started off.

"He's wounded!" Jesse said, running into the street toward Hawk. "You need tending!"

Hawk didn't look at her. The grulla trotted past her, and broke into a run. When Hawk had passed the last of the village's ragged shacks and was dropping into a shallow ravine, a thin voice called behind him.

"Thank you, Mr. Hawk!"

As he rode, chilled in his saddle and staring straight ahead, Hawk fished a small wooden carving from his coat pocket. He rubbed his thumb across the black horse rising on its rear legs and flailing its front hooves skyward, its blue-black main rippling and glistening in the snow-reflected sunlight.

Hawk brought the carving to his lips, kissed it softly, returned it to his pocket, shook it down deep so he wouldn't lose it.

Crouched and solemn, he urged his horse up out of the ravine and into the snowy western hills.

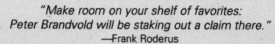